Stuart Oliver Henry

Hours with famous Parisians

Stuart Oliver Henry

Hours with famous Parisians

ISBN/EAN: 9783743311268

Manufactured in Europe, USA, Canada, Australia, Japa

Cover: Foto ©Andreas Hilbeck / pixelio.de

Manufactured and distributed by brebook publishing software
(www.brebook.com)

Stuart Oliver Henry

Hours with famous Parisians

Hours With Famous Parisians

BY

STUART HENRY

AUTHOR OF "PARIS DAYS AND EVENINGS."

CHICAGO

WAY AND WILLIAMS

1897

TO

G. J. H.

NOTE.

SEVERAL OF THESE SKETCHES HAVE APPEARED IN LONDON AND NEW YORK PERIODICALS.

CONTENTS.

WRITERS.

PEOPLE OF THE STAGE.

Contents.

Madame Adam

Madame Adam

It is not true that Madame Adam is the only man in France. The compliment would be magnificent for her, but rather whimsical.

Nevertheless, she is more masculine (using the word in a stalwart sense) than most of the Frenchmen you meet in Paris. I scarcely know a Parisian who is equipped with such a virile bearing. She is an active, brusque, business person, resolute, accustomed to giving and taking hard blows, and to deciding daily a score of important questions on the spur of the moment. She was born to command, and carries on, with unusual administrative ability, two or three secular enterprises. Among them is the *Nouvelle Revue*.

Madame Adam's photograph, with which the world at large is familiar, does not offer a correct impression of her as she is to be seen and known to-day. It is the likeness of a woman who lives solely on emotion and imagination. The face seems as if it had been washed into a certain weakness by floods of sorrow, and as if its mistress yet hoped on through the tears and despairs of life, still pinning shreds of faith and trust to the mast of her destiny.

This Murillo vision is dispelled when you see Madame Adam of an afternoon, between four and six, in her editorial room, 18 Boulevard Montmartre.* The *bureau* of the *Nouvelle Revue* reminds me more of a typical New York business office than any I have ever seen in Paris. It has a thoroughly business-like air, while most French *bureaux* have something of the atmosphere of social leisure. Its yellow oak furniture is upholstered in green; green cases of files mount to the ceiling in an orderly way; folding doors of green cloth suggest diplomacy and dispatch.

In the private sanctum of Madame

---

*Recently, since this was written, the *Revue* has changed quarters.

Adam, the walls are thinly and leanly decked with lithograph-portraits of Bourget, Loti, Heredia, with a sketch of Victor Hugo's Quasimodo, and of a scene from Molière's "L'Amour Médecin," and with colorless and unimpassioned maps of the Sahara and of the Bissago islands. An iron safe weighs the precinct down with a solid and refrigerant substantiality.

If it happens to be summer time, the window is unlatched for fresh air. Madame Adam, unlike the rest of her race, believes in heaven's fresh air. Green trees screen her from the boulevard, whose cushioned noise rides freely in through the open casement.

Madame Adam is a tall, large, finely proportioned woman. She is a picture of health. A kind of ruddy hue is on her face. Her hair is barely beginning to turn gray. Her gray eyes level a cool, steady aim at you. She wears, in her office, a gray habit with no furbelows and no ornaments save a simple medallion at her throat. Her manly shoulders are valiantly set off with epaulets. A black cord chaperons her eyeglasses.

She usually twirls or clinches them closed in her hand when she talks. Her voice is pitched in a strong, business key, and sounds as if it were straining somewhat to give proper vent to her masculine thoughts and feelings.

Since she loves to be in the thick of the fray, she is outspoken to the outermost limit. Her dominant personality probably explains why her clerks appear effaced to the pale and quaking condition of aspen leaves, for she does not hesitate to fire off such verbal projectiles as "imbeciles" and "*rustres*" in the directions where iron tonics seem to her to be needed.

She converses with admirable readiness. Her sentences are so prompt and to the point that you sometimes might fancy she had committed them to memory. There are no vague or supplemental phrases and no fumbling of words. Language, for her, is an adequate and convenient instrument. Frequently she grows eloquent in her conversation, especially when her theme is her love for France. She becomes an orator then, and has the habit of bringing her fist down on her desk, to the saltatory alarm of the various objects in the vicinity.

The religion of Madame Adam is patriotism. She is, you know, a writer on politics. She was enthusiastically initiated into their labyrinthine hopelessness by her adored friend Gambetta. Her tremendous patriotism is a source of regret to those who trust that the advent of full-righted Woman will favor peace and good-will among the modern Sabines and Romans. Madame Adam's idea is that we belong to an era of international hostility and strife, therefore one's duty is to fight chivalrously for his country, by pen and by voice, day and night, to the last breath. So, in her eyes, France is entitled to all she can get.

However, Madame Adam does not behold the workings of contemporary French politics with chauvinistic complacency. Far from that. She insists it is not true that a Frenchman can not succeed in a political career unless he hangs on to the gown of some woman. And this is, to her mind, precisely the reason why the internal politics of France are so bad.

"No," she will say, *"ce n'est pas vrai,
hélas!* for it would be better if our pretended statesmen stayed at home and list-
ened to their wives.   Instead of this, they
go to the *buffet,* to the *café,* to the club,
even.   They are a lot of *rustres* who are
looking out for their pockets and not those
of the people.   I am for democracy, on the
plan that *all* classes should be best.   We
should work to that end.   We have changed
the Greek scheme.   The Greeks went on
the idea that there should be an aristocracy
which should be the cream of a nation."

Ancient Greece is one of the splendid
hobbies of Madame Adam.   She has long been
a student of the old Hellenes, and confided
to me recently the subject of the new
studies which she is pursuing in that antique soil.   She is delving among the *mystic*
foundations of the Greek civilization.

"I hold," she told me one day, "that
the world has always stopped at the plastic
—the materialistic—glories of Hellas.   For
instance, the Athenians turned religion into
a cult, and when it becomes a cult it becomes materialistic.   People have all along

caressed the plastic beauties of Greek thought and culture, and halted at the mysticism of Plato. Now, it is just there that I begin. I am a mystic; we must reform and regenerate by mysticism—it is the only way. Christ reformed his materialistic age by his mysticism—by his symbolism. It is the occult symbolism of the Greeks that I think should be dug up — brought forth — to the light of our day.'' Herein again, in her symbolistic faith, as in her patriotic politics, Madame Adam belongs to our epoch.

She does not believe in the decadence of Frenchwomen. There are still great Frenchwomen, not perhaps just to-day, but there were a decade ago, and there will be in a few years again. She used to be taught, as a child, that she was the daughter of all who had gone before, and would be the mother of all who came after. Her confidence in her sex has been strengthened by the events and progress in its affairs during the present half century.

It was thirty-five years ago that she attracted notice by her pamphlet combating

Proudhon's dictum that women were only fit to be housekeepers or courtesans. She established the *Nouvelle Revue* to show this was not true. She had no need for a magazine. She wished simply to demonstrate that a woman could run one in every particular. And she takes a merited satisfaction in putting across its cover: "Madame Adam, Directeur"— not *Directrice*.

She has discovered, and led before the public, many persons of talent. The most famous of them is Pierre Loti.

In a word, if we had to designate the greatest Frenchwoman of our day—the one who most conspicuously maintains the traditions of the great Frenchwomen who have played, from generation to generation, a noteworthy rôle in the political, literary, or social life in France — our choice would easily fall on Madame Juliette Adam.

M. Sardou

M. Sardou

O, an actor!

An haranguer of the Revolution!

Toujours l'audace!

At his desk, he flings his arms at you, throws himself back in his chair, strikes unconscious attitudes, jumps up and strides excitedly back and forth across the room, lays down his arguments, one after the other, and under your nose, reaches down and rubs his ankles!

M. Sardou in his study, with his black velvet skull-cap, his flowing clothes, and two old Revolutionary kettle drums under the table! An agitator, a reactionist of a violent type! In his excitement, he takes off his cap, reveals the fact that he has long, silky, iron-gray hair, through which he runs his fingers and leaves it flying in the air, rams his hands in his pockets—

"*Je vais les embêter—vous allez voir!*"

He defies the Third Republic. He defies the Théâtre Français. The government is rotten, and the Théâtre Français is the refinement of decay. They must both offer him a full and humble retraction and apology on a silver platter for that Thermidor episode.

"All that is lacking is a leader. O, if Boulanger had been a little — just a little— more serious, he could have ridden from the Café Durand to the Elysée, and everybody would have cried — *Vive la France!* I am for the *bourgeois*. Let them rule. Louis Philippe — he was all right. The aristocracy reigned under the *ancien régime*, the people reigned in the Revolution — now it's the turn of the middle class. They are the backbone—the reserved force of the nation. They always pull France out of her disasters."

And the Théâtre Français! What an asylum of respectable imbeciles! Its actors can't act; its managers know nothing about the stage. M. Sardou has always found his great interpreters in the theatres of the boulevards. It was Déjazet who created his early rôles and gave him his first "send off."

"I shall never forget how I set off that June morning across the fields, with my first manuscript under my arm. I went to submit it to Déjazet. She was sixty and I twenty-six! *O je le crois bien* — Déjazet!"

M. Sardou is perfectly able and willing to take care of himself. He says to all emulators and antagonists: "The field is free and open to the world. The fight will be fair and square. I warn you I 'm a good fighter, so that if you fail or get hurt, you must not blame me." And you may be sure that, in the scuffle, M. Sardou will get the oyster and leave you the shell.

While he is so openly defiant, decided, lucid, a true friend to his friends and ever energetically at work in their behalf, he is, at the same time, smooth and subtile like an Italian. And he is an Italian. His ancestors were Italians in Sardinia.

This accounts for his love of Italy. He always spends his vacations there, or near the confines of Lombardy. Ah, yes! He is very deft, adept, Machiavelian—urbane, exuberant, unctuous.

He is delightful in his family life, and very hospitable. And he is the only playwright known to the Parisian populace and popular with them.

One's mornings with Sardou! What rousing, salient, Sans-Gêne scenes of conversation, comedy, drama, rebellion!

Déjazet—*ô je le crois bien!*

Audacity forever, young man! Audacity forever!

M. Zola

M. Zola

Always at home to you after six o'clock.

A business man. No emotion, no ideals, no imagination, no poetry, in his personal intercourse. He does not try to win or entertain you. He takes no personal interest in you, and does not expect you to take any personal interest in him.

He talks frankly and freely about everything, but in a secular way. He makes life seem to you merely a commercial career. Fiction for him is editions of 100,000 and 50,000 francs a year. His magisterial and magnificent panoramas of descriptions, unequalled for their kind, are all measured off in his mind as so many rods of printed matter at so much a rod. No one can describe a forest as he can, with its colors, nooks, grandeur, repose; but to him, individually, it simply means so many thousand feet of sawed lumber with which to

27

build emigrant vessels and dredging machines.

No personal magnetism, no sentiment, no perfume, no rose colors.

You always see him at a *vernissage.* He will be dressed like a well-to-do merchant, with his hat tipped back on his head, his fingers clutching each other behind his back, his lips moving in some prosaic conversation, his eyes seeing nothing across the crowd.

At home, after six, he is apt to wear a snug, snuff-colored, sack suit, with plenty of pockets for his hands — a close-fitting working gear. His physique is robust, with a big tendency to obesity. His voice is weak, and cracked, and pitched high. His realism finds expression in his broad nose. It is a nose constructed to root up the ground and sniff out the filth of existence.

He has a tired, overworked air. His eyes look weary, and he says "Ah!" with a sigh, when he speaks of the immense field he has rooted over and has yet to root over in his brutal manner. Life has been for him a blunt, rude, brutish thing. He has conquered merely because he has worked harder than any one else. With him, naturalistic literature succeeds only by the sweat of the brow.

And you fancy that this colossus of a novelist works fifteen or eighteen hours a day? He pretends to write only three. He begins at ten and stops at one or two in the afternoon. And his first hour amounts to little; it is only his last two hours that count.

What loins of strength, nevertheless! What Titanic capacities to achieve! He towers over all his Parisian contemporaries, as Victor Hugo towered over his epoch. Hugo and Zola are the two great French literary names of the century, for romanticism and naturalism are its two great literary movements. Still M. Zola is not strictly naturalistic, as was Maupassant. He presents other enormous attitudes and aspects. Even his severest critics confess their astonishment at his colossal enterprises — his novels with forty characters, and with immeasurable perspectives of country, history, human life.

Hugo, and Zola, his child on the naturalistic side! Four letters each and two
vowels. Both giants endowed with Hercu-
lean capacities; both excellent business
men; both hounded almost to death, and
still triumphant; both made wealthy by
their pens.

M. Daudet

M. Daudet

M. Daudet

No more delicious hour can be spent in France than that to which M. Alphonse Daudet, with his *"causerie charmeuse,"* treats his friends of a Sunday morning.

All the world knows of him as a novelist; the Parisians are familiar with him as a playwright; his bubbling gayety, gossamer fancy, perfume-pointed irony, and independent, individualistic attitude in the realm of letters, make him savored and respected by every one. Yet how few have heard of his delightful talks, of his piquant and imponderable conversation, gentle and fragile as a woman's — expansive and confiding as Tartarin's! There are in it the sparkle and laugh of Provence, the beading flavor of southern grape, the dulcet song and dance of some cascade in Languedoc.

I have just come from one of his *"causeries,"* and am able to give you the kernel of it, but not, alas, its taste and fragrance. He was saying: "No, I belong to no school. I am for the truth—that's my motto in literature. I try to picture realities. Am I naturalistic, realistic, impressionistic? I cannot say, for I pay no heed to these classifications. I was for fifteen years the dramatic critic of the *Moniteur Officiel*, and never in a single instance used any of those terms. I think that such categories and labels are for the most part useless.

"Of course, the impressionistic idea is right in one phase. Truth—actuality—constantly shift their guises—they present a different aspect to us every day, every year, every generation. Why? Because we are human beings. If we could know the complete verity and could speak of it with absolute exactness, we should no longer be men — we should be *Dieu*. In my new book, "La Petite Paroisse," I cling to reality as firmly as I possibly can in my descriptions of places and things.

"No, to my mind, this classification of literature is largely nonsense. It's like

saying this: Now the apple is round—let it
stand for round-headed people—those who
have little fancy, yet possess *le bon sens*
—the practical sense — the gift for matters
of fact. And let the pear, which is long,
stand for the people whose heads are narrow and long. The pear, therefore, represents imagination, the romantic. Then
you simply divide all writers into apples
and pears. Mr. X. is an apple; Mr. Y. is
a pear. The former has the sensibilities of
an apple; the latter is endowed with the
imagination of a pear. Mr. Z., the poet,
picks up a magazine in which there is an
exhaustive review of his works. He finds
the critic proving that he (Mr. Z.) is not
Mr. Z. but a pomological specimen — that
he has and can have no attributes except,
for instance, those belonging to an apple.
How does Mr. Z. feel about this discovery?
Why — of course, he can only feel like an
apple. I, for example — am I an apple or
a pear? I fancy I am neither one nor the
other — merely a sort of nectarine. Very
picturesque, such literary cataloguing, is n't
it? — yet what does it amount to?''

"And the prunes," I suggested, as I smiled at the thought of that famous poem, and of the rice and prune parties which Tartarin encountered in the hotel on the Rigi.

"And the prunes—" repeated M. Daudet, with a hint of amused revery, and with that genial toss of the head which is familiar to him.   .   .   .   .

"Yes, I wished to see England. What I dreaded most there was the lack of sunshine. I love the sun—I have aways missed it in Paris. We of the Midi must have plenty of sunshine—it somehow means to us health, good spirits—that things will move on better.   .   .   .   .

"I am ever dreaming even of the lands that are buried in the Arctics—I picture them to myself at night when I lie awake hour after hour, and cannot sleep. I follow in my imagination every polar expedition that starts on its journey—I see in my mind's eye, day by day, the brave, suffering explorers as they toil wearily over the ice and snow.

"Yes, I am always reading books of

travel—always. No country is too distant
to pique my constant curiosity. It is not
difficult to understand, then, that England,
with its mists and green lawns, has ever
held a large place in the realm of my fantasy.

"I have never been a great traveler in
reality, but I am an indefatigable one in my
fancies. You know I went to Algeria before I put together Tartarin — I had seen
Africa before writing the book — I went
with a friend — "

"And Tartarin?" I queried.

"And *I* was Tartarin."   .   .   .   .

"No, I may almost say that I went to
London without any preconceived notions
about the English. Of course, I would not
be frank with myself if I did not confess
that I had never liked an Englishman.
Still, I had not known one English person
well — and had met very few English people; in fact, I think I had only met them in
traveling.

"I must admit that my experiences with
them *en voyage* had never been happy — perhaps it was partly my fault. When I was
on my wedding tour an Englishman was

with us in the compartment in the train. I
wanted the window lowered — he insisted
that it be kept closed — I explained that
my wife needed fresh air — the window remained shut. Finally, in a fit of impa-
tience, I thrust my elbow through the pane,
and exclaimed: 'There, sir, keep the air
from entering now, if you can!'

"Of course, my southern nature is expansive, confiding — the British disposition is
not naturally of that type. It has been my
idea that the *fond* — the foundation — of
an Englishman's temperament or character,
is *ennui* — and that is why he is so hospitable in his home, and so ready to welcome
strangers to his fireside.

"But my dislike for the English has
changed during the past three years. My
books have been selling well in England —
the London people have said the friendliest
and pleasantest things of me. All that has
had its effect; and this, added to my admiration — which has always been great —
for the world-wide power and civilizing influence of that dauntless isle, made me
very curious to visit it. . . . .

"I am not doing anything for the theatre now. I am not as much at ease in drama or comedy as in fiction. To succeed with a play, you must be a debater, a kind of protagonist — you must have unabashed confidence in your opinions about the stage, so that you can say to the manager and actors: 'You must do that — the public wants this!'

"That is not my nature. I listen to those around me, and think that other people must be right, and do as every one else suggests. The trouble with the theatre manager is that he is under great stress. His expenses are heavy, and he is always striving to *faire le maximum*. As I know nothing of the 'maximum,' I promptly yield to his judgment. Still, I have had some very good ideas about the theatre. Porel was exclaiming only the other day in reference to a certain play, 'O, if I had followed your advice!'

"I have done a great deal of critical work across the footlights. I was the first in Paris to insist on a more elaborate and scientific *mise en scène*. Sarcey came after

me in this. I was the first, too, to write
a history of dramatic criticism in France.
I traced the links of its evolution down to
Napoleon I. Napoleon was, in point of
time, our first dramatic critic. He studied
plays and the audiences in something of a
systematic way, and began to introduce
method where all had been caprice and
chaos. He integrated the theatre — he
commenced to convert it into an organized
factor in public and popular education and
life."

"Do you think," I queried, "that the
café chantant is really making inroads into
the domain of the theatre? Is the *café
chantant* of Parisian origin, or does it come
from southern France?"

"O, the *café chantant* is a French institution — it comes from all parts of France.
Take our village inn of an evening. Some
one is called upon to sing or recite. When
he is done, a lounger cries out—'*Et vous—
là-bas* — give us something; it 's your turn.'
This invited one responds, like his prede-
cessor, with a selection — so the evening

passes off. Everybody contributes from his repertory.

"That is the beginning of the *café chantant*. It is in vogue in Paris because it is cheap — you can smoke there, and talk, and you do not have to think. At the theatre, on the other hand, you pay a big price for a narrow, uncomfortable seat — you can't move nor chat, and you have to think to follow the play. The *fond* of the spectator is *indolence*. He wants to sit on the small of his back and be entertained, with the least exertion possible on his part. The Frenchman is active, nervous — he does not like to listen more than three minutes at a time. He wishes to turn to his neighbor and say, 'O, I have heard that song rendered better down in the Rue ——; I can render it better myself' — he wants to chatter and sing. This kind of temperament is death to the theatre, and is the life of the *café chantant*. It explains why the concert hall is so popular with us.

"And then you cannot hear the actors distinctly nowadays. There is only Coquelin who has a voice — an *organe*. The rest

are great, but they are too old, or have lost
their teeth, or speak with their backs toward you.   As for me — I say it frankly —
le théâtre m'assomme—the theatre is a ter-
rible bore to me.

"Music,— O, that 's another matter!   I
adore music — orchestra,   voice,   piano,
street organ, jew's harp — I patronize them
all — yes, and Wagner, too.   I was a Wag-
nerian long before he became the fashion
in France.   No, I never met Wagner, but
I will tell you this.   One day an acquaint-
ance of mine was in Wagner's *cabinet de
travail* at Baireuth.   Among the portraits
hanging there, he was surprised to discover
mine.   'What!' he exclaimed, 'why here 's
a Frenchman!'   'Yes,' responded Wagner,
'I am fond of Daudet — he is the only
Frenchman I would have in my house.'

"Do you know Henry James?   He is always kind enough to come and see me when
he is in Paris.   I find him charming.   I
do not read English — unless it 's about me
— but he is said by my friends to hold the
highest rank as a novelist in England and
America."

"Yes," I replied, "I am told the only criticism usually offered on him is that his style is prolix — parentheses, dashes, semicolons, all chained together in one sentence.

"O, if that is so, I think this is the explanation: he is a great lover of Flaubert — is a competent authority on him — and has fallen heir to his style. We have, in general, two kinds of literary style in France; that of Voltaire — brief, limpid sentences; and that of Chateaubriand and Flaubert — long, flowing periods that never end. Flaubert used to recite whole pages of Chateaubriand — he was passionately fond of passing through his 'gueuloir' those immense, unrolling panorama-paragraphs.

"There is Flaubert right behind you—an *eau forte* — that is just as he looked. And Turgeneff? Yes, he was one of our four — I was deeply attached to him, *mais j'éprouvai un déboire.* You remember what I have written about it. Turgeneff accepted my hospitality here, and I supposed he was one of my truest friends, and still, as you know, he was writing in his souvenirs that I was utterly devoid of character and talent.

Many Russians have come to see me, and have said that it could not be so, that such dissimulation is not possible to the Russian nature, and so on. I don't know — *enfin, c'était comme ça* — no one has ever been able to explain away what Turgeneff left in his memoirs.

"But the 'Jeunes' have all that is new and curious to-day. The young men naturally hold the coming generation in their hands. It is a strange and significant fact that they look upon Baudelaire as a kind of godfather. I knew Baudelaire well. He lived at 46 Rue Amsterdam, and I at 44. I used to be with him every day — we ate together frequently — he called me '*mon petit.*' He was thirty-seven, and I was eighteen. After a while we rather avoided each other, or, at any rate, I tried to avoid him. What displeased me most about Baudelaire was his posing. For instance — we were walking one morning past a great block of dismantled buildings — an ugly mass of ruins. Baudelaire stopped, beheld it fatalistically, and exclaimed in a dramatic way: '*C'est la destruction!*'

"Is it possible that, as you say, foreigners in Paris complain of the *vie fermée* of Parisian households? Why, the idea had never occurred to me. I do not understand it. You see how it all is about you here (throwing his arm in a careless gesture) — how unpretending it is — old things. We live in modest comfort — friends, acquaintances, strangers — all are welcome — every one does as he pleases. Of course, at the same time, we lead a close family life. I was laughing just before you came in, for I heard my boy of sixteen ask his mother, 'Won't you go walking with me this afternoon?' 'I cannot — I must take your little sister out — why do n't you go alone?' 'O, I do n't want to go without you.'

"My eldest son lives in another part of town, but he comes here every day in the year to embrace me, and to inquire, 'How are you to-day, father?' '*Moi, je suis pour la famille*'—I believe with my heart and soul in the sanctity of marriage and the fireside. I am not in favor of the institution of divorce. Love of family and love of country — those are my two great mottoes. It seems to me ideal to choose one person and to say to yourself — 'That is the person whose eyes I am to close forever, or who is to seal mine in the last sleep.'

"When you visit us at Champrosay this summer, I will show you that *our* family life is by no means *fermée* — walled up. With us, every one makes himself at home. We get together at breakfast time — we stroll into the park — we shout to each other — we wear our old clothes — we give a rendezvous for five o'clock tea — we talk, laugh, sing. My son has a tennis court there. I go and sit on a bench, and watch the game. A photographer in the Avenue Victor Hugo has photographed the scene. There I am with my cane, and with a big hat drawn down over my ears. I look like a patriarch — they call me the 'old man.'"

Callers are announced. I reluctantly take leave of the *cher maître.* I pass out of the ebony-colored apartment in the Rue Bellechasse. The furniture is antique — the furnishings are dark — a *jardinière* of red cyclamens saucily perk up their heads on a table—two or three of J. L. Brown's pictures enliven the walls. And I come away filled with the charm of a delectable hour — a charm that somehow suggests the moral refinement of Sully Prudhomme, the grace of Raphael Collin, the delicacy of Puech.

* * *

M. Daudet is so delightful that I cannot resist the temptation of ringing his floor whenever I am in his street. If he likes you, the valet will always open the door for you to the study without hesitation or ceremony.

One morning last month as I burst in on him in this fashion, he was fumbling over some books and papers on his desk and was ready, as usual, to talk of everything. He picked up a little volume at his right hand, and said: "Do you see that? I'll tell you what it is. It was sent me by the author — who he is I have n't the slightest idea. But see — the text is only printed in the middle of each page, so that there's a large white space above, below, and on each side of the type. I use it for writing memoranda. Look, how I've written data all over its leaves — very convenient — I use it every day for my notes. I call that book a practical example of the æsthetic spirit."

"But the poor author?" I hinted.

"O, as for the author, why I have written him thanking him for thinking of me, and told him that his book is always on my desk — it never quits my sight."

To be besieged by all kinds of people, and requests, and missives is one of the disagreeable features of being a celebrity, especially if you are known to have a warm heart like that of M. Daudet. Here are two samples of the letters which he receives almost daily. He was reading them to me that morning. The first was composed in poor French by an American woman. It ran as follows:

"CHICAGO, April 5, 1896.

Dear Sir:—I have your new book, "The Little Parish." It is very good. Indeed, it is all the talk around here. Now, I should like to give you an idea. Why not write a novel about the New Woman? I think that would be a splendid subject for you. Yours truly,

CAROLINE W——."

Why was that letter written? you ask. Merely to capture M. Daudet's autographic response. But in this instance the writer had shot too wide of the mark.

The second letter was dated "Berlin," and was written in good French and in a Spencerian hand. It was long. This is a fragment of it:

"You old villain! You are like all other Frenchmen — too mean to live. You have no conscience, no sincerity. You are utterly incapable of telling the truth or writing it. You should be taught a handsome lesson — you, and your race as well. And you can rest assured that the Germans are keeping a sharp eye on you all, and at the first opportunity they will visit Paris again; but this time it will not be on round trip tickets. They will stay for good. You ought to be hit with a bullet; and if some one does not do his duty by you, I, myself, will see that the deed is done."

This is, of course, some poor, demented person who has as yet escaped the asylum. M. Daudet does not know who he is any more than you or I. Still, it is not pleasant to receive such a *billet-doux* over your morning cup of coffee. And to think that this should fall to the lot of the genial, generous author of "Jack"!

In illustration of these qualities in him, let your fancy witness the following little scene which happened one Sunday morning when I was in his studio. A letter was brought in. M. Daudet eyed the signature, and skirmished over the contents, mumblingly quoting the phrases, "My misery is about to end"— "At last hope gilds the future" — "I need but five francs."

M. Daudet turned to us, saying: "Ah! if we could be sure that his story is true!" He slipped a five-franc piece in an envelope, sealed it, and sent it out.

Then he read the letter to us, and said: "There is a whole novel here. Three or four years ago, I received a copy of a periodical from Languedoc — a wild-eyed sheet proclaiming the resurrection of literature, the reform of the French language, and so on. It was hoarse with 'Down with modern methods!' — 'Death to the contemporary *littérateurs!*' After a time, the editor appeared on the scene in Paris. He had come to carry the war into Africa. He

did not have air enough in Montpellier.
But Paris and Montpellier are not the same
thing. He had made a great noise down
in his province, but here his reverberations
were swallowed up in silence in the great
roar of Paris.

"So he almost starved. He came to me,
because he knew I was from the south. I
helped him a little. He has kept along,
barely able to cling to existence with his
wife and child — no work, no money, no
friends. Finally, to-day, he writes triumph-
antly — as you have heard — that he has
secured the position of spy on the police
force. He is to 'run in' thieves and track
suspicious characters. 'My misery is about
to end' — 'a light is beginning to break.'
His expansive, exploding, southern nature
is enthusiastic over the glorious prospect.
The lowest post on the detective service of
Paris is for his grateful soul *la gloire*—fame
and fortune. Four years ago, nothing
short of reforming language and literature
from beginning to end would have satisfied
his lofty ambition. And now he is elated
over the chance of being a Paris police

scout, at a salary of a hundred francs a month. Ah, Paris! This is not the first ardent, immortal, magnificent soul you have extinguished in your slums. You are grand and beautiful, but how many mortal careers you may have to answer for — sometime — somewhere!''

M. Catulle Mendès

M. Catulle Mendès

For nearly forty years he has been one of the most conspicuous figures of the sensational belletristic and social world in the French capital. He was scarcely more than a boy when he impetuously joined the ranks of the young Parnassians. He did as much as any one to form them into a company, and to-day he is still waging, with all the fire of his quondam adolescence, the battle of the Parnassians against the later schools and movements.

Early in his tempestuous campaign he established the *Revue Fantaisiste*, which ceased to exist when he was fined and imprisoned for having published, within its covers, a poem whose allurements offended the notice of the public censor. Then, in 1866, he married Mademoiselle Judith Gautier, the daughter of the poet; but they separated before very long, and reverberations of the famous incident filled the air in Paris for several years.

M. Mendès has long taken an especial interest in Wagner. Wagner was a contributor to the *Revue Fantaisiste* at the time of his unsuccessful débuts in Paris as a composer. But it was not until later that M. Mendès commenced to champion Wagner's musical cause in France. One of the merits of the rôle of M. Mendès is that he faithfully fought the Wagner fight to its finish in Paris. By pen, by word of mouth, by editorial and by *conférence*, he has all along exalted Wagner in the teeth of a hostile public.

This has been one feature of his ardent cult of Art and Beauty. "The love of glorious Art and Literature" is the almost excessive passion of his soul. It is not his fault if the arena of modern French letters has not been a satisfactory scene of tournaments, duels, galas, banquets, adventures, and exciting occurrences of every kind. For, a trait of his disposition is the capacity to furnish "incidents." If a play of his is refused at a theatre, the affair is somehow converted into a small *cause célèbre*. He is prone to find, in personal paragraphs, offenses which would escape the attention of other people. In such instances, he courts duels by sending forth Hotspur notes like this: "Messieurs, the items which you have been gratuitous enough to publish about me are false. If you did not mean to be personal, you were badly informed; otherwise, you are imbeciles." If he is invited to read a poem at a banquet where such moral dignitaries as Messieurs Bérenger and Brunetière are present, he is sure to create an "incident" by mischievously emphasizing the refrain — *Et ce cher Baudelaire.*

In short, his life would furnish more materials for a melodramatic literary chronicler than that of any of his *confrères*. And still he is an indefatigable — prolific — writer. Some fifty volumes and plays owe their existence to his pen. He has poured forth poems, novels, *contes*, dramas, comedies, addresses, prefaces. A facile and elegant artisan of prose, he is likewise an adept chiseler of verse. He has written of

boudoirs de verre, of love confessionals, of
the hygiene of beauty, of the songs of
France. His tales of his Colettes and his
Luscignoles are prettily decked out in silks
and satins, in blue and rose. His Spanish
serenades are rhymed with a richly decorative virtuosity. But out of all his productions, and as a result of his long career,
what will remain?

He has answered the question as follows:
"A few volumes preserved, because of
their dedications, in the libraries of the
friends whom I leave behind; two or three
poems—or merely a sonnet—in the anthol-
ogies; and also perhaps—a chimera of
which I sweetly, gloriously, dream sometimes—my bust in the 'Luxembourg gardens full of roses.' O, by no means so high
nor so large as that of my beloved guide
and master, Banville. My pride rises to
strange heights when my devotion to poetry, not my own output, is placed in question. My greatest satisfaction comes from
the fact that, through all the misfortunes,
the joys, and the agitations of life, I have
fulfilled—unfailingly and with enthusiasm

—my literary duty. It is this that I love
to be praised for. My grandest delight is
to read a beautiful page and to cry out to
everybody that it is beautiful."

M. Mendès is of medium size. His hair
and beard are of a soft, brown hue, and
silky. His manners are graceful and rather
showy. Occasionally you see him at the
National Library in the Rue Richelieu.
When there, he engages the attendants to
bring him armloads of books, he begins to
make a few notes, friends come, and, in
his quick, nervous way, he hurries off for
the day, and forgets to accomplish that for
which he came. At a *première*, he often
appears with his hat and clothes rumpled,
his beard untrimmed, as if he had been in a
lost mood for a week.

He has described the miserable hole in
the wall where he was stopping when, one
winter morning, years ago, a pale, timid
youth named François Coppée was ushered
in, and their long acquaintanceship began.
There was one chair, a *lit de sangle*, a grate
without fire, poverty, a very pinched hope
of success or notoriety. At present M.

Mendès is *chez lui* at Chatou, that favorite suburban village, which lies between the winding gray ribbons of the Seine and under the terrace of Saint-Germain.

*   *   *

Time: seven o'clock in the evening.

Place: the white and gold Glacier Napolitain on the grand boulevards, opposite the Vaudeville.

People are drinking absinthe.

M. Mendès, with his hat off, and in his best Bohemian style. His audience is composed of three men, and a handsome, mystic-haired young woman, who looks beatific and says nothing. M. Mendès's gestures of flow and fervor have mown a swath around him. He has energetic periods, and then soft, suave passages, wherein drips the dew and blooms the rose. His Parnassian cadences are redolent of perfume and nectar.

He is talking of England. "I saw surprising things there. Imagine this: At a famous college near London — can't recall the name — they were holding the annual exercises. I was present. They played

a piece of Plautus in Latin, a piece of Aristophanes in Greek, and a scene of —
"Champignol malgré lui!" Would you
have believed it? And in England! Astonishing! I was surprised, too, to find Jane
Hading's picture in all the students' rooms.
She is the great favorite there. Strange,
is n't it?

"I had the honor of presiding at a college banquet. The chief spokesman
warned me at the table that he was going
to toast me in Latin and that I must pay
him back in coin of the same stamp. I
have never pretended to be a Latin scholar,
but I scribbled off some notes and read
them in response. As the English accent
of Latin is entirely different from ours, I
got out of the scholastic scrape all right. I
did not understand a word my friend said,
and no one understood me.

"Most Frenchmen find London a sombre
bore. Poor Georges Courteline wept all
the time we were there — cried for Paris.
But I had a royal time — was handsomely
entertained. The Thames scenery is not
to be surpassed. What beautiful, verdant

vistas stretching away to skies of mellow gold! What luxury of landscape, fit for the romances of the Knights of the Grail! London seemed to me simply an immense long village that never becomes a city. You say to yourself: 'It is not attractive now, but at the next street it will be magnificent!' It always remains a big, homely town. . . . .

"I am astonished at the littleness of contemporary literary genius in France. In my opinion, it is due to our military régime. To pass three years in the barracks, is the literary death of a young man. Look at Germany! She has long had the military régime, and has had no one since Goethe. We began imitating her system after 1870, and now we have the same blight. I have just received a letter from a young friend who is serving his term in camp. He is in the depths of despair. He is afraid he will have no talent of any kind left. . . . .

"Yes, I know some consider me a facile and prolific writer, but do you know it is the hardest thing in the world for me to write? I lock myself in my study soon after noon. After having smoked and idled about for an hour, I commence work. The first sixty minutes I can do little. It seems as if I can never get to the bottom of the first page. Afterward it goes along better. I stop at five or six. And the remarkable thing is that writing becomes harder for me the older I grow and the more I write. Now, to-night, I am to do thirty lines for the *Journal* about a little play at La Cigale. You cannot believe how those thirty lines haunt me. I do not feel now that I can possibly do them. I have n't the slightest idea what I shall say. I assure you I am thoroughly unstrung about it."

The subject changes to Wagner.

"I recall, as if it were yesterday, the first time I met Wagner. I was a stripling of seventeen and was launching the *Revue Fantaisiste*. It was in 1861. I was looking about for talent — for contributors. A friend told me of Wagner — Wagner was then in Paris — and gave me some of his verse. I saw in the author just the kind of material I wished. I was anxious to get

him to collaborate with us in the *Revue*.
My friend took me to call on him. Wagner
was living on the second floor, I remember.
When we went in, he was at work composing and writing at the piano. I made known
my wants.

" 'Do you know my music?' he asked.

" 'No,' I said, 'but I have read your
poems.'

"He made an earnest gesture, and replied, like a symbolist:

" '*C' est la même chose*' (it is one and the
same thing).

"A beautiful response, was n't it? I shall
never forget it. '*C' est la même chose.*'
Beautiful! Significant!

"We were ever after the best of friends.
About ten years later my wife and I went
to Lucerne and passed three months with
him. Villiers de l'Isle—Adam was with us.
Those three months were the happiest I
have ever known. We stayed at a hotel
near Wagner's villa. Villiers and I walked
about a great deal. As we strolled, the
people took off their hats and bowed rever-

entially to us, and Villiers would turn to me and say:

" 'What the devil is the matter with these imbeciles?' "

"We found out at length that the king of Bavaria was expected on a visit — 'incog' — to Wagner, and the Lucerners had mistaken me for the king, and Villiers for Prince — Somebody — his companion.

"Wagner worked mornings. We joined him at two in the afternoon, and spent the rest of the day with him. We often found him in his wrapper at work — playing the piano with his left hand and jotting down notes and words with his right. He was very methodical — regular in his habits. They may say what they please, but all men of genius are like that.

"What an entertaining host — Wagner! I have never seen his equal — hospitable, open, enthusiastic, informal. He took us all around Switzerland, and we could hardly succeed in spending 50 centimes. He paid everything. He had the best rooms in the hotels engaged ahead, and all bills receipted in advance. We had the choicest of everything. Nothing was too good for us.

"Opposite the Grutli, he said to us: 'Rossini was the most voluptuously endowed of all composers.'

"Wagner was then fifty-six or fifty-seven years of age, and the greatest romp you ever heard of. Often, when he saw us coming, he would jump out of the window of the first floor into the garden, in order to welcome us the quicker. Villiers was playing ball with Wagner's dog one day, and the dog accidentally bit him in the hand. Villiers had to go about with his hand tied up. Wagner pretended that the dog was mad, and that Villiers was a victim of hydrophobia. Sometimes when Villiers and I entered the garden, Wagner would run to the nearest tree and climb it in playful pretension that Villiers was an enraged creature seeking whom he might devour. A perfect tomboy!

"Wagner was the most amusing, charming man I ever knew. The days I passed

with him have been the best of my life.
What a grand and simple soul!

"I have always tried to tell our French
people this, but they called me a 'Wagner-
phobe.' "

M. Paul Verlaine

M. Paul Verlaine

I shall try to give you the little scene in the naturalistic style — not through the prisms of imagination nor the spectacles of moralization.

Place — Café du Soleil. Time — half past five p. m. I have come here to get a glimpse of the greatest living *French Bohemian poet (unless you care for any reason to except Richepin). I have brought along, as a Bohemian companion, Richepin's abominable "Le Pavé," which has been loaned me by a Bohemian student. In the corner nearest Notre Dame is Verlaine. I sit down at a stand just opposite him — ten feet away — and pretend to be reading my book. His faithful glass of absinthe is at his right hand. He has as yet merely sipped of it. It is too early in the day for him to be drunk. He is engaged in

*Written not long before his death.

writing, smoking an old pipe, and reading newspapers. He glances up and down the columns of the journals in a rather keen, energetic fashion, as if seriously eager to glean their contents.

Ablack slouch hat is drawn down over his ears. His coat collar is turned up, for the weather is not warm. He has on a dark blue coat, muddy-hued trousers, low shoes and grayish socks.

His spectacles ride the end of his nose, and whenever he looks away, he looks over them. His moustache and beard are grizzled, ill-combed, dirty. To judge from his rather full face, one would say that he is in a good state of health. His eyes are small and bright. They twinkle — snap — with intelligence. Their color seems to be a bluish gray. His nose is *retroussé* — very. The back of his neck and head — reflected in the mirror behind him — has evidently just been cared for by a barber, and presents a trimmed, oiled and prosperous appearance.

He looks his age — about fifty. Every few moments, he lays aside his newspaper, and writes several lines. Then he resumes his reading. At a stand at his left and a little in front of him — not more than four feet away from his face — are three men drinking absinthe, and keeping up a quiet disturbance. Two of them are young — one a well-dressed, fine-looking fellow. The third is about fifty-five, and is a type of that Latin Quarter Bohemianism which one sees around the Place Maubert and at the Père Lunette. He is a stale *gamin* who would have been a fit subject for Gavarni. The old codger's face is unshaven and unwashed. The well-dressed young man, with playful rudeness, slaps him on the cheek and pours a glass of water on his bald pate.

Verlaine laughs at their performances. The old *gamin* tries to kiss Verlaine's hand in veneration — Verlaine resists — the gaffer finally succeeds. He closely watches Verlaine write. He takes one of the written sheets and begins reading it. Verlaine gets up and snatches it back, exclaiming: "*Laissez-moi çà!*" (Let that alone.) He continues his scribbling, but keeps an amused eye on his frolicking neighbors. At a stand at his right are four or five students and two or three *filles* (girls) of the Quarter. One of the girls is red-cheeked, pretty, and is sporting an attractive toilet. She is smoking a cigarette. She comes over to the Verlaine party. The well-dressed young man clasps her in a long and ardent embrace — lips to lips. She sits down in front of Verlaine, and orders a gum absinthe.

In fifteen minutes the Verlaine group breaks up. He lifts himself from his seat, puts his "flying sheets" in his pocket, and leaves on the table his writing equipment and his absinthe. He limps toward me with his cane, and shakes hands with a man who is writing verses at a stand just at my side. Verlaine scans him: "Trying to compose something that does not go?" His voice is low, soft, pleasant — that of a man of culture. He looks at me and laughs a little, as if he half understood that I, a newcomer in these haunts, was watching him. He slowly drags his diseased leg

past my table with difficulty and some pain.
I see his clothes near at hand — they are
poor and soiled. He hobbles along, and
every one in the café manifests deference
and respect toward him. He remarks that
he will soon be back — and moves out of
the front door.

Such is an hour passed with Paul Verlaine in one of his three homes — café, hos-
pital and prison. He will return here to
this café in half an hour, spend his evening, get drunk, and his Bohemian friends
will help him reach his bed in some miserable den of darkness. To-morrow afternoon he will come back for the same programme.

This is the daily life of the celebrated
Bohemian poet of Paris — of the stanzaist
who has touched the rigid French rhyme
with the rarest of delicate and vibrant gestures — who has found incomparably dainty
shades and tints in the rhythms of the
French language.

He is the author of "Sagesse," which is
composed of some of the most genuinely

religious — Christian — verse known to French belles-lettres. But he is more famous, perhaps, for having written some of the most depraved poetry known to any literature.

M. Coppée

M. Coppée

He lives right among some of the humble people he loves so well — away at the south end of the Faubourg Saint-Germain — Rue Oudinot 12. It is a ward that looms with hospitals, and shines with the gilded summit of the Hôtel des Invalides. This fact perhaps explains in part why hospitals and the Invalides figure so abundantly in the verse and prose of this famous writer on whom we happen to be calling this morning.

We enter from the street into a poor court which suggests chickens, a midwife always "of the first class," and a thrifty *concierge* who is betimes a tailor. Likely a great cat will be lounging about in a lordly way, for M. Coppée is fond of cats. What a plain doorway, this one at the right where we are ringing! And what a loud, clanging noise the bell makes! It is a one-story house and seems very low and small. The door opens, and we traverse two or three rooms which are modest, but which glisten from scrubbing as if a Dutch servant were about the place.

We find the poet in a red dressing sack —staringly red. He is smoking cigarettes, of course, and habitually throws a stub into the grate by way of emphasis to an exclamation point or a period. How he makes one feel at home! As he talks, he sits at his desk, or lounges on his huge, inviting sofa, or walks back and forth or up to you and away. His conversation smacks of the Paris *chronique*, and the current popular words are in his mouth — a little very effective and picturesque slang included.

His cult of the Humble is genuine; he feels at home among them. Still this does not prevent him from being sought after in the aristocratic salons of Paris. He will be saying, for instance:

"Yes, I have been pretty sick — caused by catching cold at the Princess Mathilde's the other day. O, I suffered terribly — I

do n't know what the doctor really thought
—perhaps he thought I would not pull
through. And I am so busy nowadays,
too. You know I 'm one of the *pauvres
diables* who have to earn their bread with
their pens, and can't afford the luxury of
being sick long. It 's hard work, this pen
work, but I 'm thankful that I have to de-
pend no more on a little government position where you just earn enough to live
and a little too much to starve, *vous savez.*
O, I served in that *galère* for several years.
Mon Dieu, quelle corvée! They ask me if
it is worse than the publishers. Yes, I
know about the publishers. We authors are
resigned in France, despite all their abuses,
real and imagined. But what can be done?
Nothing—it 's utterly useless to kick out
of the traces. There has been only one
French author who made publishers do as
he wanted them to do—handled them with
an iron glove in fact—that was Hugo.

"Personally, I have no complaints on the
subject. You see I dabble in several different literary genres. Now and then the
Théâtre Français or the Odéon takes a

drama from me. Then I write my
chroniques for the *Journal.* Then there
are my stories for newspapers and maga-
zines. And then my verse. I have several
strings to my bow, poor as they may be. I
do n't think I write as much poetry as I
used to — perhaps it does not bring in as
much money as the other things. And
then I was fond of the *romance* — songs —
but the *romance* has become rather old fash-
ioned in France. The modern *café chantant* songs — the *chat noir* songs — all that
is the mode to-day. It is *rigolo* as the boys
say, but of course it is n't poetry.

"I am ultra with respect to many important living questions. I know I write much
that many people only dare to think. But
I 'm not a '*progressiste*' in all things — in
the matter of the reform of French ortho-
graphy, for instance. O, *par exemple!* I
cannot stomach that. Think of such a
massacre as that would be of our classic
French verse — six masculine rhymes following each other, and all that sort of
thing! How much do we really care because many people can't spell well? When

I was a young man and used to get love letters from the girls, did I love any one of them the less because she wrote me, *Je thème*, instead of *Je t'aime?* Not a bit of it. I remember writing a poem once about a sweet little blonde whom I was fond of at the time, and in the poem I insisted that—

'J'aime tes fautes d'orthographe.' "

In this free and easy style M. Coppée runs on. He is frequently taken for a commercial traveler in the country hotels where he stops when out in the provinces of France. He loves to idle about in the hotel offices and smoke and tell stories with everybody. Very fond is he of the little theatres in the suburbs of Paris — in those places of humble entertainment where human life and character are seen in their plain and naked truth. In such resorts he finds the incidents and types which he can weave into *contes* that draw tears from mild eyes. In that simple class of life he was born and reared, and he is ever happy to revert to the days of his insignificant youth. It reminds one of the charming remark of Delphine Gay: "You always keep a little

of the political opinion you had when you
were a pretty woman.''

As we sit here in the study of M. Coppée
and look at his books and pictures, and
catch, through the window, a glimpse of his
little garden, we think perhaps of his latest
chronique—that one which we were reading and laughing over yesterday.　It
rambled on in this way:

"Yes, I have seen many public fêtes, and
still I am not very old.　May 1, 1847, was
one.　I was five.　My father carried me
around Paris on his back, poor man.　When
we were over by the Tuileries, Louis-
Philippe came out on the balcony, and
everybody shouted, '*Vive le roi!*'　In a
year he had to fly from town in a fiacre.　I
was so young I did n't know much about
it—I, with a corner of my shirt appearing
through a hole in the rear of my *culotte*.
In 1848 I saw the Tree of Liberty planted
near our house.　The godmother of the occasion was Julia the Oyster-Opener.　She
opened the oysters in a neighboring inn,
and did not have a reputation as a dragon
of virtue.　When I was a starving govern-

ment employee, I utilized the fête days in running out into the country with my little '*connaissance.*' I never had any money of my own for gala occasions, but I had a big silver watch on which the Mont de Piété used to lend me fifteen francs. So she and I would go and dine at Vélizy's — in that green arbor where the spiders drop into your soup."

M. Anatole France

.

M. Anatole France

M. France is a delicious philosopher and lover. His novels charm especially the *Parisiennes*. The delicate cut of his paragraphs, the cologne of his sentiment, the calmly disquieted grace of his philosophy, trail tremors of curiosity and aesthetic satisfaction through the hearts of his feminine readers.

M. Bourget has become too difficult, complex, abstruse for women. He has lost, to a great degree, the enraptured favour of those Paris ladies who love to skim and dip the wings of their literary sensibilities in the surfaces of French fiction. So, M. France is probably to-day the favourite romancer of these dainty dames. You find the reason for it in his savourous simplicity —in the relish of his not attempting astonishing — immense — feats as a novelist.

And, personally, M. France merits his

renown.   For,   the   belletristic   Frenchwomen rave about him—about the enchant-
ment of his conversation and manners.   He
knows how to satisfy their desire for melli-
fluous courtlinesses of attention, how to perfume their thoughts with emotions, how to
add vistas of old gold and richly faded scar-
lets and purples to the realms of their fancies.   I have seen *Parisiennes* fold their frail
and scented fingers in pinnacles of beatific
despair in their endeavors to express the
delight they have experienced at the hands
of this indolent skeptic.

The industrious indolence of his nature
spreads a veil of repose across his chapters.
His cult of doing little is aristocratic and
artistic.   He toils at what he pleases—at
novels, to be sure, but only when the mood
bids him.

Then there is restfulness, too, in his
mildly agitated and optimistic skepticism.
It is light, yet amazingly daring.   He says
the most unexpected, revolutionary, "impossible" things, and they have such a certain aspect or measure of truth, such a per-
suasive and delectable indifference, that

you do not rebel. On the contrary, you
let, with resigned pleasure, your consciousness be titillated by the entertainment of
the surprise — of the unconventional bold-
ness — of his religious *dilettantisme*, for example.

I have used the "word religious," since M.
France has contributed to the religious evolution in recent French literature. Religion — ascetic, aesthetic, erotic — is a main
subject with him. The epoch which he is
especially fond of is the Preraphaelite. The
passions of the saints, the erring caprices
of nuns, monastic purity and elevation
along the severe, vertical lines of the Fra
Angelico art, freely tempt the courteous
fervor of his notice.

The little villa which he has recently
taken possession of in the Villa Saïd is decorated with art objects of the Preraphaelite
and post — Preraphaelite centuries. There
are quaint and prim pictures of the Van
Eyck school, old carved oaken doors from
Tours, ancient chimney mantels from
Venice. There are, too, Italian ceiling
pieces that recall, with their rosy cherubs

and gay, flowered designs, the bridal chambers in the hostelries of Lombardy.

To return to the personal subject of our portrait. Of the literary men I have met in Paris, M. France has, in truth, the most elegant presence and style. Their polish would almost seem overdone were they not relieved by his moods and gestures of vague indulgence and unfinished ease. He is clothed in an abundant suavity, in a soft luxury of bearing. He has a mellow voice of gold. His large, liquid, dark-brown eyes bespeak his gentleness. He is *doux*, infinitely *doux*, the French say.

The curious feature of his social intercourse is that he now and then forgets you and himself, and floats into the mystic domains of his thoughts and fancies. Fascinating indeed is this quietly ecstatic spectacle of a man who is absorbed in you and in your modern topic of conversation one moment, while the next finds him utterly oblivious of the present, and away off in another clime, in another age, pursuing some Thaïs vision or some Platonic theme, as he treads the incense fields of his romanesque imagination.

I have seen him escorting visitors, with all his devotion of genial courtesy and interest, from his study to his street door in the Villa Saïd, and suddenly wandering into some room under the wand of a momentary whim, and wholly disappearing from view. His callers were by no means offended. They were charmed thus to fade from his attention without the awkward *ennui*, the graceless friction, of a goodby ceremony. He had already forgotten that he had been interrupted — that his forenoon had been half lost. It is this amiable haze of Lethean revery, this sweetening impressionistic atmosphere of poetic ideality, that he makes vibrate across his pages of subtile speculation and aromatic irreverence.

Although M. France has a reputation which is compounded of the literary and the social, and is truly said to be the chief attraction in one or two of the Paris salons, he will deny to you any social rôle whatever. He will remark: "I made the tour of the world of salons — a sort of Sindbad — a few years ago, and then retired into my den. I wished to ascertain what they were like. One has to do that kind of thing in France. I am fond of solitude, and I do not pretend to photograph with my pen the types and affairs of real life. The nervousness connected with the effort of writing causes me to court isolation. I have no *cénacle* about me. If I had, I should not admit it, because that would imply a subordination in those who come to see me."

M. France is scarcely fifty-five. Among the young literary men of Paris he has only friends and admirers. Among the older men he has three or four enemies, but they are charmed enemies.

M. Jules Lemaitre

M. Jules Lemaitre

M. Lemaitre is not tall. He is compactly built. His vivid little bluish eyes scintillate from a well-developed head. He has high cheek bones, and a short, thin growth of reddish whiskers. His hair is turning gray.

Although he works in an *atelier*, he is never a painter or a sculptor: he is always a literary man. He writes with his face toward the great glass front of a light-flooded apartment dignified by lofty tapestried walls. "Yes," he will say as you take a seat by his desk, "I like light — plenty of it. And I am fond of walking to and fro, a cigarette in hand."

Books are piled on his table in such a manner that he is left small space for writing. A terra-cotta bust of Renan casts its mild eyes over the unpretending *pénates* about you, while behind it six or seven bas-reliefs are hung in a row, two of them representing Goujon's nymphs of the Seine. Below the bust will be leaning perhaps a bicycle, for M. Lemaitre is a devotee of the wheel. He will soon bid you come and see his little garden. You follow him through a tiny *salle-à-manger* and then through a tapestried fumoir half-full of large green plants. The miniature, square, high-walled garden, with its six or seven trees, looks beautiful in June. "I work out here a great deal in the warm season," M. Lemaitre will remark. "I am a son of the soil. I was born in the Loire valley, you know. I have a place of my own there where I go every spring, and stay as long as my duties in Paris will permit. . . . I adore the country," he will repeat in his quiet, abashed way.

It is difficult to conceive that this subtle critic, this dainty and scrupulous play-wright, this Parisian master of sentimental psychology, feminine scepticism and refined irony is, and will ever remain, a kind of peasant — a man from the country. Reared in the provinces, and faithful to his early companions of earth, grass, foliage and skies, M. Lemaitre affects little of metropolitan polish and facile fencing of manner. He is slow, and not sure of speech; he has a habit of nervously folding his hands and raising them toward his chin; and he indulges in an embarrassed, suppressed laugh. Yet while he is a proletaire, — a rustic, — you never discover in his pages the sunlight, the fresh air, nature, the populace. His literary temperament, his intellectual qualities, his moral susceptibilities, are typically and admirably Parisian in every signification of the term.

If you ask him about the contemporary French theatre and literature, he will say he believes that the "young reviews" of Paris are regarded with too much importance by foreign critics and writers. He will express the fear that his plays are not adapted to English audiences, since they are written for a rather eclectic boulevard public, and probably will never find a soil to flourish in outside the national capital. He will explain his regret that he knows no modern language save his own. "I am

well equipped in Latin, and fairly so in
Greek. I tried to learn one or two living
tongues, but when it came to mastering a
vocabulary sufficient for practical use, I
confess I had not the courage for the task.
And, furthermore, I was educated during
the Empire, and under religious auspices.
Modern languages were not then the fashion
in France." The long and thorough aca-
demic training of M. Lemaitre throws light
on the fact that analytical and subtilizing
processes elbow out of his varied productions any distinctly original creations and
exotic conceptions. "Yes," he will observe, "I shall give myself almost wholly
to the theatre. I hardly think I shall write
hereafter any sketches of my contemporaries. Every time I publish one I make an
enemy." He will accompany you to the
door in a modest, shy way that would lead
observers to suppose that *you* were noted,
not he.

And such is, at home, that witty con-
noisseur and clever *dilettante* and scholar
who, more than anyone just now, is influ-
encing French fashions and tastes in the

matter of the drama. His impressionistic
species of dramatic criticism is in full vogue
in Paris nowadays. His style is everywhere
delicate, graceful, entertaining, irrespon-
sible. He neither attempts to seize the
utmost nor embrace the whole. And yet
he has as much as anyone a nervous and
alert curiosity. He lives on sensibilities,
and not on plastic and mobile beauty like a
Parnassian. He is a psychologist — an
adept and cautious dissector with scalpel in
hand. In discussion he is virtually unan-
swerable, for he always says: " It is true
that I am not able to comprehend you — so
much the worse for me." To anyone who
violently assaults his books and literary
methods, M. Lemaitre, like M. Anatole
France, humbly responds: " I deeply regret
that Monsieur X —— despises me and de-
tests my works. He has me at an immense
disadvantage, since I frankly confess that
I am a great admirer both of him and his
writings." As Monsieur X —— can never
claim with good grace before the public
that this is irony, he can only lapse into
silence before such polite geniality.

M. Lemaitre was not constituted to relish vast souls. Dante, Shakespeare, Goethe, Hugo are *menus* too tremendous for him. His tastes are those of the daintiest gourmet. The smallest *plat* seems too large for his appetite. The great *table d'hôte* plans of learned thought and speculation frighten him. He shuns the long, exotic bills of fare of every kind — Tolstoiism, Wagnerism, preraphaelitism. It is true he endeavoured to season Ibsen to the French liking, yet, afterward, he rather pushed away that Scandinavian dish from his own sight.

Thus, the influence of M. Lemaitre is of a genuine Parisian stamp. And, for similar reasons in part, it is practically confined to the things of our time. Unlike his fellow critics, he has not tissued his reputation out of studies of past epochs. It is a fabric woven of the life around him. He is infatuated with *to-day*. No French writer has prized and praised our abused generation as much as he. Yet, strange to say, he has not identified himself with, nor welcomed, those contemporary impulses and modes called symbolism, mysticism, *déca-dentisme.*

Actuality was the gist of his claim upon the favor of the French Academy. His "Contemporains" is his most valuable production, since it is the most complete reflection to be found of the present French epoch in so far as the epoch is Parisian. On the other hand, as a monument of professional criticism, it equals the work of neither Brunetière, Bourget nor Faguet. It is too lackadaisical and amateurish, as the author himself would be first to avow.

The present was the natural and proper background for his impressionistic talents to play upon. As is well known he stands for the impressionistic method in the art of reviewing. The times were ripe for this method, and around and about it there has grouped a sort of school to which belong, in reality, the young and serious French critics. Hence, the position of M. Lemaitre as a commentator is incontestably important.

And he has virtually carried impression-

ism to the stage, for, while his comedies
have failed before the public at large, they
have proved of marked significance to re-
viewers, and form a noteworthy factor in
the complex equation of the French theatre.
Doubtless, the future will witness him at
his best as a playwright, since he intends
gradually to confine his efforts to playmak-
ing.   It is, therefore, safe to assume that
his series of dramatic comments known as
" Impressions du théâtre," will become
more and more diluted.

The personality of M. Lemaitre is greater
than his productions; and his style is more
interesting than his ideas, for you do not
think of him as having ideas. His language
is pure French and yet the most modern.
It is impressionistic prose, *ondoyant et chat-
oyant.* Atmosphere vibrates across it.   It
pulsates with vitality.   His paragraphs
dance before the eye with the nervous
piquancy of *pointillisme.* Graced with a
woman's temperament, M. Lemaitre has
the feminine gift of saying the merest anything in a diverting manner. And he freely
heightens his effects by little vistas en-

livened with the pyrotechnics of brilliant paradoxes.

His individuality has been enriched by the variety of existences which he has led. For he was first a peasant, then a kind of youthful religious recluse, then a *Normalien* and a professor in the provinces, and finally a *Renaniste* and a literary artist and *dilettante* in Paris. More than any of his critical *confrères* does he typify the average Parisian of our decade. He believes not, and yet is incurably inquisitive about everything that is new and French. He is a tolerant and amiable skeptic, a genial ironist full of malicious indulgence, a critic who smothers his victim into silence with criticizing compliments, and who gently tries to destroy his adversary into immortality.

As a censor, he annihilates nothing, champions nothing, explains nothing. He simply appreciates. For him, truth does not exist because it constantly transforms. Facts appear to him so unstable and elastic that they are only fit to leave fleeting impressions. He has discovered that statistics and great arrays and perspectives of

thought and feeling are always disproved
and illusory. He has learned that the
present belies the past and that to-morrow
will gainsay both. Why, then, should one
take the empty trouble, as a critical scholar,
to attempt colossal age-defying structures
on the sand plains of time? And he has
answered the question for himself by his
impressionistic cult of to-day.

On this account he is the most popular of
the French critics, for the masses are only
interested in their own generation. His
" Contemporains " is seen on the book
shelves of all the little *foyers* of Paris. He
has vulgarized his themes in a refined and
entertaining way. In his critical volumes,
the careless, general reader is served
to autobiography, revery, sentimentality,
esprit. These books are five o'clock teas
where the author is pleased to *tutoyer* his
guests, and to make them enjoy their host
at the delicious profit and flattered expense
of their absent friends. And he laces up
now and then his scrupulous *nonchalance*
with a consummate paragraph, or an expert
excellence of some kind, that causes one to

exclaim with regret, " Ah, if he would only keep trying!"

The prevailing element of timid disquietude in the composition of his temperament is counteracted neither by a romantic imagination, nor by a soothing love for history (i. e. the past) as in the instance of Renan, nor by a fondness for philosophic calm as in the case of M. Anatole France. The restlessness of M. Lemaitre, due primarily to his life of inner sensibilities, is therefore more extreme than theirs. It is hyperaesthesia. He finds no sure and quiet place to lay his head amid the world's endless whirlpool of vain appearances and illusions.

Hence, his existence would be a torture to his readers and himself did he not repose his nervousness on the pillows of irresponsibility, and dip the fingers of his excessively analytical consciousness in the pleasant surfaces of mere impressionistic sensations. If he believed, with M. Brunetière, that the critic should have an apostolic mission, an accountable duty, constantly to perform, he would go mad, for, having

no faith in self-assurance or mortal infalli-
bility, he would be harrassed to death by the
thought that he must *prove*, and by the fear
that he had not expressed the *whole* truth
and had not been *perfectly* just.   This is the
fundamental reason why his pages teem
with *pasticcio* remarks in the style of everybody, and why he frequently bursts in
through opened doors and gallops down
upon deserted camps.

The nature of the influence and literary
product of M. Lemaitre is thus both logical
and self-contradictory.   In any comparison
between him and his critical colleagues, he
appears nearest the truth in these days
simply because he flees the notion of its
absoluteness.   He affirms nothing and ac-
cepts all.   He denies nothing and treats
everything with a cautious reserve.   In
affecting no philosophy, he is most a philosopher.   He has no Christian faith, and
still possesses a genuine religious spirit.
He is a kind of diaphanous mystic, and yet
does not look with favor on mystic cults.
While he is the most elegantly frivolous of
his *confrères*, he is, nevertheless, the most

tender and human. He is the most capricious and evaporative of them all, and still he is the one who penetrates our inner selves with the most delicate and titillating directness and whose presence seems to linger with us the longest. He walks the prudent ground of practical, every-day life, and yet he is the most sentimental and fantastic of any of his emulators. He is a Parisian of the Parisians, and still, as you see him at a *première*, he is apparently the only countryman in Paris save M. Sarcey. For, as a rule, he is carelessly dressed, his hat is ruffled, his beard untrimmed. His back is vaulted like a ploughman's, and he always shuffles about myopically and ill at ease. He is fond of effacing himself into a corner with a friend and slyly whispering and laughing in a screwed-up, microscopic way, as if he had just been stealing a march on some overweening agricultural neighbour.

In M. Lemaitre, the Academy accepted little else than a *fin de siècle* soul. But it is an opal of the rarest iridescence.

M. Huysmans

M. Huysmans

A quiet apartment in the palace of the French Minister of the Interior. A room furnished in green, a large desk, one or two sheets of paper, plenty of leisure, nothing apparently to do. The window open, a glimpse of green branches, a silent April afternoon.

A quiet little man at the desk. His legs are crossed and he is fumbling a ruler. His small, pointed gray beard and mustache are neatly clipped, and his gray hair is geometrically trimmed à la Renaissance park of Versailles. His cranium bulges out at the sides. He has a rather bright eye and a squirrel look.

Not a suave, facile man of the world. A noiseless talker willing to talk, but not knowing what to say next. No ceremony, no enthusiasm, no parade. A part of the time he scrapes the desk with his ruler like an idle boy at school.

He chops out the conversation something like this:

" It takes me two years to '*document*' myself for a novel — two years of hard work. That is the trouble with the naturalistic novel — it requires so much documentary care. I never make, like Zola, a plan for a book. I know how it will begin and how it will end — that 's all. When I finally get to writing it, it goes along rather fast — *assez vite.*

" My business is applying naturalism to Catholicism. I have become a Catholic because I am extremely pessimistic. The religious people differ from the other pessimists only in that they annex a 'future life' scheme. Everything is going to the dogs. There is a great deal in the church that is a fraud. Its miracles, confessionals — all that is claptrap and absurd. But I enjoy its old preraphaelite spirit, its high animus, its art.

" In my next novels I shall study church paintings and cathedrals. Just now I am at work at the cathedrals of Chartres and Rheims. I am studying everything about them — stones, altars, windows. The only thing left for a novelist to dig into is Catholicism. The relations of the little grocery girl with the proprietor of the wine-shop on the corner, have been thoroughly exploited. Nothing remains untouched but Catholicism and its art. The priests are *bête* — they have killed religious art — we have none nowadays.

"The symbolists and neo-realists are a rather poor lot, in my humble opinion. There can't be any idealism in all that. The only effective idealism is in church mysticism. Brunetière is right: Science is bankrupted. This is the only thing in which I agree with him — and I don't see how that has happened. Science won't make us happy. But that does not prevent Zola from being the greatest of them all. What a tower of might!

"The psychologists are too artificial — necessarily so. They can't tell the whole truth — they can only tell it in a polite and varnished way. *Mon Dieu!* the old church writers could beat all the Bourgets and Anatole Frances put together."

All this, and more, is said in a low tone
of voice, in an echoless, independent, reck-
less way, without gestures or flourishes.
M. Huysmans is serious, quizzical, rever-
ential, Bohemian. He mixes religion, slang,
indifference, realism, mysticism, hope, despair — all — in a determined but tranquil
air of convinced *insouciance*.

M. Drumont

M. Drumont

A lurid editorial sanctum at night. A fiercely red grate fire. An ominously shaded red lamplight. A nervous occupant—a human firebrand in flesh. His black beard and masses of wild hair agitating in violent excitement. His feverish, red-rimmed eyes smokily bespectacled. His hirsute hands flinging in the air. Jumpings up and down. Leapings to and fro. Seethings, hissings, boilings of rage, hot, sulphurous emissions of revenge. A fandango of Vesuvian frenzy. Fire-eating paradoxes exploding across scarlet cataclysms. The echo of terrorizing *c-r-r-aquements*, *débâcles* — the Jews, the priests, the aristocrats, the Rothschilds, the *rastaquouères*, the vile Republican plutocracy — *oui*, *Messieurs* — they will all come to direst grief, not next century but this century, to-morrow, perhaps this very night. The

masses are ready. The word will be said
— the match lighted — and you will see
what will burn up, *c-r-r-r-r-ouler*, disappear.
Money — that tyrant of the ages! *Ah!
Messieurs*, the worm turns under the heels
of the miserable despots. They nearly
crushed out the people, but, thank God!
we shall have the future. The past can
belong to that hydra-headed conspiracy.
What care we for the past? It is only
synonymous with an infamous compact —
the Jews mortgaging homes, the politicians
mortgaging rights, the church mortgaging
souls. The priests could not be the pawn-
brokers, so they turned that trade over to
the Jews. The church blessed the rich in
order that they might share their gains
with it and securely keep the rest. History
is the record of the party of the first part.
Its "progress" is based on two per cent. a
month. Its "civilization" is the product
of usurers and courtesans. *Oui, Messieurs!*
In the Middle Ages they scared the people
into submission by threatening hell, the
devil, religion. Nowadays they try to scare
us with jails, guillotines, the law. But a

new dawn is at hand. There will be a new
day. And what an awakening! I feel it in
my bones! It will amaze you — it will amaze
me. It may be bloodless — it may be the
bloodiest revolution ever known — who can
tell? It may be death to you and to me,
but let it come —*dies iræ*— for it will be
Justice! The Shylocks will have to pay at
last. Everything foretells it. Scandal after
scandal! The perpetual falling out of the
thieves among themselves! The solemn-
faced *farceurs* wrapped in the cloaks of
law, order, conscience! How they will
dance to the music of bombs! The Jews
will dodge the petards on the pavement.
The *bourgeois* will hide his head under his
bedclothes. In vain! No one — nothing
— will escape. The wolves at our throats!
Think of the millions of poor devils of men
without bread this very moment! Starving!
Begging crumbs from the plutocrats! I see
it every day of my life — you see it — men
asking the privilege of working on a dung
heap. And this has been true of countless
generations, protected by the law, blessed
by the priests; and they would silence us

by proclaiming that it is the mysterious order of Providence! They are taking our last sou to-day. We *must* act. To-morrow where shall we get a morsel of food? The dogs will lick our misery in the streets, and the rich will roll by in their rubber-tire vehicles and smile at us and drink their wine out of human skulls. Do you suppose this is going on and on? That our sons will always black the boots of these monsters and our daughters always be their concubines,— to stop hunger from gnawing? *Jamais!* Rather a thousand times the peace of death to-morrow — at once! The kid-gloved blackguards — the diamond-spotted villains! They have ridden to the edge — they will ride no farther. What a Dance of Skeletons when it comes! It will be for some new Orcagna or Holbein to paint — this *fin de siècle* Brumaire — this Damnation of the World - Faust — this apotheosis of blood, debauch, crime, chaos —!

M. Hervieu

M. Hervieu

It was a September evening at Saint Germain — Rue Voltaire — under the frowning heights of the old chateau. M. Hervieu was there *en villégiature* that year. A quiet town; a quiet street; a quiet apartment with the glass doors closed that led into the little graveled garden, for the chill of autumn was on the air.

The servants appeared and disappeared without being heard. The dinner was not hilarious or vivacious. A comfortable stillness haunted us over the black coffee in the smoking-room, while M. Octave Mirbeau told stories of priests, and M. Remy Saint-Maurice detailed curious incidents of Paris life, and M. Hervieu mutely and leisurely punctuated the course of the talk with characteristic comments.

All was silent, restful, agreeable. The accents and accords of sound fell to a muffling floor. And the late train slipped back to Paris in stillness.

Our host, in his noiseless way, seemed to have masked the occasion and muzzled the night. . . . .

M. Hervieu is one of the five or six great figures among the French writers who are between thirty and forty years of age. He is brainy — in appearance, the brainiest of any young Frenchman I have met. His cranium is very visibly laden with gray matter. His striking head — striking for a sort of veiled massiveness — easily dominates his rather slight body. His grayish eyes are heavy, slow, far away. He has a look of intellectual solidity — indeed of thickness, of denseness, using these terms in a favorable sense. A sad muteness speaks from his motionless lips. His handwriting, as I see it in a note lying before me, is compact, tortuous — there is something of a blind cast over it. He is by nature neither hopeful nor convinced. He wears a silent air of sadness — a breastplate of sentiment — for he is a pessimist. The spectacle of civilization has no bright windows of faith for him. Not that he does not believe that the human race has progressed. But it takes so long — so long.

M. Hervieu is apparently a student both in attitude and action. His head is pushed forward from his shoulders; his neat, thin fingers seem to caress each leaf with bookish fondness as they slip between the pages of a volume in quest, for instance, of a citation to prove an argument.

He lives in the Rue Auber by the Grand Opéra, right in the center of that Parisian life which he loves to contemplate. In his study you hear the dull, ceaseless roar of carriages sweeping past on the wood pavement. His books are piled around the room in a sort of precise disorder, and his desk is so encumbered with material that the smallest place possible is left him for writing.

He talks to you there with an echoless earnestness, folding his hands between his knees and perhaps around a white handkerchief, as he leans toward you. He spoke to me one day of his almost abnormal passion for observing men and things. He said: "If an accident happens in the street, I rush forward, mix with the throng, and stay. I drink in the scene with quenchless thirst. This passion for watching the world makes me indolent. I put off writing until the last moment — until I am forced to take up my pen. I have to toil under stress. As a result, I write a novel in three months, and then am ill two months. I began 'L 'Armature' the 4th day of October, 1894, and finished it January 20th — two attacks of gout being included in the programme. You see I had to commence furnishing the copy December 15 for the *Revue des Deux Mondes*. I worked from eight till noon, and from one until six. Insomnia? No, fortunately, I am a valiant sleeper. This fashion of working is bad for the health, still it has some advantages — it gives the fever of life to your pages — your hot blood flows into them.

"I take no notes (save mental ones, of course) in preparing to write a novel. No, I do not put living people in my books. A lady said to me the other day: 'I know every person in 'L 'Armature!'' 'Do you,

Madame?' I replied. 'You are more *au
courant* than I, for I was not aware of having painted any one in reality.'"

The talent of M. Hervieu consists primarily of his powers of observation and his
forcible style. He always conceives the
general plan of a book before he attempts
to confide anything to ink. He first makes
a full outline of it on paper and then goes
over the outline and converts it into better
French. He finds that his mind uncon-
sciously stores up many data, details, impressions, so that for his purpose his pen is
ever well enough provided with material of
this sort.

Of the symbolists, M. Hervieu is not a
disciple. He thinks that classifications into
schools in literature are merely convenient
things with which to cudgel our literary
adversaries, and nurse the comfortable
notion that "only my friends and I have
genius — and even my friends . . ."
Every one, though, is to some extent a
symbolist. What is M. Hervieu's Baron
Safre but a colossal symbolic figure?

M. Hervieu was born at Neuilly, adjoining Paris, in 1857. He was educated for the law and also for a diplomatic career. In 1881, he was appointed Secretary of the French Legation in the city of the Montezumas. Thereupon, he gave up diplomacy, together with the Napoleonic code, and went into fiction.

M. Hervieu is not only a great novelist, but a great playwright. "Les Paroles Restent" met with a highly satisfactory reception at the Vaudeville in 1893, and the Théâtre Français has welcomed to its repertory his "Tenailles."

*   *   *   *

A general rehearsal at the Théâtre Français is interesting because of two classes of people you see there. There is, first, the class that everyone in Paris knows, at least by sight. It is composed mainly of actors and actresses and dramatic critics. Perhaps nothing can be said of these celebrities when observed together, except that they look much older than their public photographs.

Then there is the class of unknown, nondescript persons whom no one ever sees unless at general rehearsals. They are curious types of the French race. They appear to have come from odd retreats in the country or forgotten nooks in the suburbs. They are provincial cousins of the author, obsolete *littérateurs* and neglected actors of two generations ago, who, in their antiquated garbs and with their rococo faces, seem to have stepped forth from the pages of old French fiction.

At the rehearsal of "Les Tenailles," you would have been struck also by the contrast between the white, burning, sunlit world on the outside of the windows, and, on the inside, an artificial world of wrinkles covered up, and faded complexions flamboyantly decorated. The contrast was as painful as suggestive. The everlasting battle against old age! Every one appeared no longer young. Powder and paint did their utmost, still the sun cruelly revealed the fictitiousness of it all.

No one knows at what hour a general rehearsal at the Théâtre Français will begin. That of "Les Tenailles" was vaguely set for half-past one. We waited, waited, and

the three curtain-rising knocks were heard
at length at half-past two. But so rapidly
was the piece played that we were on our
way home at half-past four.

The subject of "Les Tenailles" is the
French divorce law. In this play, M. Hervieu wishes to picture the dreadful existence
of an honorable man and wife whose characters do not accord, whose temperaments
are absolutely dissimilar. Yet they are
forced by law to live with each other: the
tenailles of the statutes forever grip them
together. Formerly, in France, they could
have been divorced under a "mutual consent" act which was this in effect: A
discontented married couple might lay their
case before a Judge, and he could say,
"Return in a year, and if your decision is
not altered, I will pronounce your divorce."
But the famous author of the present French
divorce law, M. Naquet, was unable to per-
suade the Senate to accept the "mutual
consent" feature. Hence "Les Tenailles"
of M. Hervieu.

One of his characters arouses applause

by insisting that marriage should be an involuntary act. The three great events of life are birth, marriage, death. Nature, he says, brings us into the world and takes us out of it without our wish. Is it not logical to believe Nature means that, likewise, we should be married involuntarily?

The audience applauds also the following passage: The old brother-in-law complains of being worn out with having to rise at five each morning for the hunt. He must be punctual at rendezvous, he must to bed early — no liberty, no repose, no pleasure even. "Can you not take a day's vacation?" asks his wife. To which he replies impatiently: "If it were work, yes; but since it is amusement, impossible!"

* * * *

We do not usually think of the French novelist as having a huge and virile sort of genius and talent. Notwithstanding the traditions of Hugo, Balzac, Flaubert, Zola, we associate him with delicacy, artistic charm, the feminine. When there springs full-armed into notice a young Parisian

romancer who is powerful, epic, and free
from the taint or meshes of sexual enamour-
ment, a rare thing has happened.

Such was the case of M. Hervieu on
the appearance of " L'Armature." His
"Peints par eux-mêmes," it is true, had
attracted notice. It contained "L'Armature" in a very fair state of development.
It has the same theme of *mondaine* and
erring misery, the same *tournure* of characters, with Baron Munstein becoming the
future Baron Safre. Yet, while " L'Armature " has fortified, magnified, consecrated
all this, it displays in full force and effect,
for the first time in the history of French
fiction, a puissance of make that is metallic
and is as if welded by a *preux*. It was
written by a pen held in a hand of mail —
by a kind of mediæval knight whose
humanity throbs underneath a thick coat of
armor.

The redoubtable author finds that the
basis of our nineteenth century civilization
is not armor, as in the Middle Ages, but
another metallic substance—*money*. Money
is the "armature" of metal which holds

together and preserves the form of the less solid duties, principles and sentiments which are the expression of society. It was fitting, then "that 'L'Armature'' should have been written in a metallic style.

M. Zola has "bâti" the French peasant, and M. Hervieu has reared in Parc Monceau the colossal golden god of money.

M. Hervieu exemplifies the qualities which M. Brunetière has glorified in pessimism. According to the latter, a pessimistic soul is strong, wholesome, noble, because it disdains this world and realizes the pitiable misery of man. Therefore, it should be more disposed than other souls to aid, to ameliorate. M. Hervieu believes with Schopenhauer and M. Brunetière that life is bad, that man is bad, that the tomb is truly a liberator. And, as already indicated, there is likely no other literary person in Paris whose face, bearing, attitude, voice, give such evidence of a profound and innate hopelessness. Constantly mingling in society, he has confessed assiduously its members so that, like a priest, he sees only good in death. He has not a

whit of a reformer's enthusiasm. Being
clean of the intrigues, iniquities, culpable
indulgences which characterize society as
he observes and presents it, he is openly
hostile to vice. He recognizes its power
and longevity, so he does not encourage.
He describes ruthlessly the various social
evils, and stops there. This is the nature
of his moral attitude, aim and influence.
For the transgressing characters of his
books, he has the tenderness of silence.
He neither indoctrinates, censures, nor vul-
garizes.

M. Hervieu once told me that he did not
see why he should not be considered a
naturalistic writer. And it is quite true
that naturalistic qualities predominate in
his later volumes. "Toutes observations
et reflexions dans L'Armature sont person-
elles de l'auteur." Perhaps we seize most
clearly some of the traits that classify him
by noting wherein he modestly differs from
his grandfather in literature — Balzac. M.
Hervieu is never a mystic, a romanesque
being in the clouds, as Balzac was at times,
and we have remarked that he does not put

into his pages people who live in the flesh
like Père Goriot or Vautrin. But, on the
other hand, M. Hervieu has in his novels
the dramatic gift which Balzac did not
possess, and shares with him the fatalistic
instinct. He can place his characters on a
pedestal, and clarify, intensify, enlarge his
situations. He can hurl forth sentences
with the force and shock of a cavalry charge.

M. Hervieu is the first French naturalistic novelist to work and be at home in the
aristocratic domain. Balzac was very ill-at-
ease there and Zola has avoided it. The
tendency of the naturalistic writer is to
haunt the middle and lower classes, and the
psychologists court the upper classes — the
vie mondaine. M. Hervieu, while he has the
brutality of a surgeon, shuns, like the psychologist, grossness, bestiality, as these
terms are commonly understood, for they
do not characterize the world which he
lives in and depicts. Since he is not a
sentimentalist, he does not blend environments into the souls of his characters.
The surroundings in which his personages
exist are fully described, yet in an objective

way. Their moods, unlike those of Madame
Bovary, find no expression in the inanimate
world about them — in landscape, sea, furniture.

In a word M. Hervieu is in no sense
poetic, æsthetic, idealistic.

He writes with a distinctly philosophic
plan and purpose. He always strikes for
the motive that controls, for the impulse
behind. He is a generalizer to whom a
thing is not so valuable for itself as for its
relation to something else — to whom a per-
sonage is only interesting for the universal
passion which he visualizes. Hence he
attacks avarice, not the avaricious; he
attacks, not censurable lovers, but *mondaine*
love which, according to M. Anatole France,
has acquired, with civilization, the regu-
larity of a game whose rules the men and
women of the world observe.

M. Hervieu has a rather picturesque, if
cuirassed, style. Especial notice should be
called to his verbs. They grip and clinch
in a grim, crushing manner. He has been
set upon by the grammarians for his diffuse
rhetorical crudities. He justifies himself

by saying that he is searching new forms of language that better fit the life and needs of to-day. And his protagonists M. Brunetière and the *Revue des Deux Mondes*, defend him in these words: " Des choses nouvelles s'expriment d'une manière nouvelle comme elles; et on ne dit rien d'un peu profond dans une langue banale."

The first productions of M. Hervieu had a simpleness of manner, and were pervaded by a genuine *personal* emotion. He has since become, because of his grandiose, intellectual, drastic, metallic talents and style — the Brunetière of French novelists.

M. Henri de Régnier

M. Henri de Régnier

M. de Régnier is about thirty-three years of age, and has lived a silent life in the quarter of the Trocadéro. He is very tall and slender. His figure and face are melancholic and fatigued. His heavily-arched eyes look far behind and beyond one. He affects a monocle which gives him a dandified air wholly foreign to his retiring and reflective nature. He discusses contemporary literature, in private or in a salon, with a sensible modesty and a *terre-à-terre* reserve. He regards Baudelaire as a perfect symbolistic poet, and finds that Hugo is full of symbolism, only that it is undeveloped — being left, as a rule, until the last two lines of a poem.

The maturer *brochures* of M. de Régnier form the one important and durable poetic product thus far yielded by the young symbolistic school in France. One reason why this school has met with slow favor among the French is that its general tone is profoundly mournful. Since its main aim is to illustrate moral and fatal truths, its most effective symbols are those which have been admonitorily, ruefully, associated with man throughout the whole troubled course of history.

The temperament of M. de Régnier is not only mournful but almost funereal. He is prone to display his sentiments "parmi les pompes mortes," and to trail his imagination under skies of ink. The cause of this is not a Baudelairesque malady, nor a broken-hearted love as in the instance of Sully Prudhomme, nor a robust and wrathy pessimism as in the case of Leconte de Lisle, with his resplendent tropics and gorgeous pageantries. M. de Régnier is simply a quiet, contented optimist whose melancholy is the mark and expression of his personal happiness. He is an æsthete whose luxury is elegiac and sombre.

His sadness, which has, he says, three friends: Yesterday, To-day, To-morrow, takes the flight of time as its all-embracing text. This text is a variation of that of "la Légende des siècles" and the "Emaux et Camées." The great and solemn theme of the four-volumed "Légende des siècles" is the pitiful smallness and perishableness of human works, whether gigantic pyramid or monumental forum. And it is well known how the grave and microscopic Gautier exhorted men to defy the ages by working in marble, bronze, enamel. But M. de Régnier folds his hands as if idle and helpless, watches the hours move by, and enjoys the regret that the past melts into the far distance, since space and time heighten the effect of his pleasurable sorrow. He is in no sense a realist.

The unique and exquisite satisfaction which he gives his reader is derived from the skill with which his consciousness of fleeting time is dissolved into music, it is true, yet also, and more specifically, into a liquid flow—a fluidity of verse. In his pages, the static art of Gautier, of Leconte de Lisle, of even Hugo, is found flowing along in a kind of poetic solution with little hesitation of period and with little friction of rhyme. Clearly indisputable are the legitimate value and charm of his conservative "vers libre" whenever its liberty of assonance, of alliteration, of lost rhyme, suggests with flexible felicity the voluntary marriage of metrical form to sentiment. Illustrative of all this, is his little poem

LES OMBRES DES HEURES.

Viens! la douceur de vivre éclòt dans nos pensées
Et les Ombres avec les Heures sont passées,
Une à une, portant à leurs mains, une à une,
L'argent clair de la coupe et l'argile de l'urne
Avec des palmes d'or et des grappes de roses,
Et celle-ci menant devant elle, ivre et fauve,
Par les cornes, un grand bouc noir barbu de roux
Qui mord un bouquet vert de ciguë et de houx,
Et celle-là passant le long de la colline
Et près du lac, parmi le cortège des cygnes,
Et celle qui riait et celle qui pleurait,
Et celle qui semblait sortir de la forêt,
Et l'autre qui semblait s'en aller vers la mer;
Et toutes, tour à tour, sur l'Orient plus clair,
Avec la coupe, avec le bouc et avec l'urne
Et les palmes et les roses et une à une
Disparaissaient, laissant, lentes dans nos pensées,
Le sourire en passant de leurs bouches lassées.

Here, where the symbolistic virgins of Puvis de Chavannes glide through aërified expanses, and where the scene speeds deliciously on and on because the poet is not checked by full punctuations nor restrained by the necessity of polishing the axles of rigid rhymes, there is, too, a graceful example of his synthetic gift, for he renumbers and regroups, at the close, his various trailing figures and emblems.

Since the synthetical is an essential feature of the symbolistic art, the ideas treated by a symbolistic poet tend to the utmost simplicity and generality: he would banish the particularities and accidents of epoch, *milieu*, and events. This was one fact which converted M. Brunetière to a lenient regard for the serious promises of this young, anti-naturalistic school, for it is the "général" in literature which attracts his attention and admiration. His rather vague dictum that symbolism has reintegrated "l'idée dans la poésie" should not be interpreted, then, as meaning that the vital interest of the symbolistic versemaker depends on ideas.

M. de Régnier, in composing a poem, does three things. He takes, for instance, his favorite theme of the flight of time, and fixes to it an image like that of fleeting water. These two parts of the task are always simple, for he selects with indifference both the idea and the image. To work them into an allegory, is his real and difficult undertaking — the true symbolistic feat.

As with Gautier and Leconte de Lisle, it is still the exterior guise, the envelope, the principle of art for art's sake, that concern him, but his æstheticism, unlike theirs, is liquid and weds the pulsating flow of the soulful and the human. The self-imposed duty of M. de Régnier is to give an enigmatic appearance to this exterior guise, and to make it thereby significantly mysterious and obscure; he must mask his thought, his colors, his effects, and never name them. This he did in an unrelenting manner in "Poèmes anciens et romanesques." His incomprehensibility — the inevitable tendency of any emblematic effort to poetize the indefinite and indefinable — is less latent in his riper books, "Tel qu'en songe," "Aréthuse." .

Naturally, he traces his poetic lineage to Mallarmé and Baudelaire, and through Baudelaire to Hugo.   Nevertheless, in his first *brochures*, there is to be remarked the direct and undisguised authority of Leconte de Lisle — a taste for the classic and a sense of stationary, magisterial size.   In the evolution of M. de Régnier into symbolism, his Greek "sites" and Renaissance parks have transformed into more imaginative, allegorical, magic vistas, and his unicorns, amphoræ, cortèges, are no longer meaningless decorations, but reflect emblematically a sentient interior and ulterior realm.

It is due to the influence of Leconte de Lisle that M. de Régnier entered into the Greek pantheistic domain rather than into that of the truly romantic and Rosicrucian. As a result of the blending of these two domains — of avoiding the plastic materialism which is characteristic of the one, and of sacrificing the Christian element which is characteristic of the other — his poetry assumes a certain preraphaelite, De Chavannesque aspect and interest.

M. de Régnier has been notably inspired

by the dramas of Wagner. He considers Wagner an important poet whose new note was the humanization of mythology. The ability and decided talents of M. de Régnier have been admitted all along, even by rigorous Parnassians like his father-in-law, M. de Heredia, and by Sully Prudhomme, who both have deplored, of course, his obscurantism and his " vers libre." One reason why the young poet has succeeded in bringing his polymorphous verse through to a triumph, is that he has been wise enough not to break with every tradition, but to respect his classic, and time-consecrated, literary ancestry.

M. Marcel Prévost

M. Marcel Prévost

The famous discoverer of the Demi-Virgins of Paris!

A young novelist of thirty-three! A man of the world! M. Paul Bourget is his ideal. Woman and love are his themes.

His pages are impregnated with the aroma of woman, with the perfume of amber and fern. The eternal feminine forever pursues him. His fiction is of the romanesque type. If you ask him to name a romanesque novel, he will name the "Lys dans la Vallée" of Balzac. M. Bourget has said that M. Prévost began, in this kind of literature, where George Sand left off.

What a *froufrou* of curiosity the title of his novel the "Demi-Virgins" trailed across the public conscience in Paris! Hermaphrodites and hybrids are always disquieting.

What is a Demi-Virgin? According to

M. Prévost, she is, as a class, much more
frequent in other countries than in France,
for "flirting" is an Anglo-Saxon device;
and you may garland the word with all the
poetry and innocence you please, yet the
whole truth is known about it.   M. Prévost
says: "Abandon the modern notion of
giving girls a liberal — a universal — education.   Teach them not life as it is, but
duty, honor, resignation.   Hurry them back
into convents to be piously instructed there,
or the institution of marriage will perish."

The Demi-Virgin is, then, a girl who
amuses herself in the society of men.   She
leads an elegant life; she is luxuriously
entertained.   She competes with young
women (i. e. her seniors) and disputes their
title to their admirers with the insolent
advantage of her fresh youth.   She exercises
over the daughters of the respectable
middle class the same sort of influence that
the club man exercises over the college
student.

The Demi-Virgins of M. Prévost flute
the verbiage of *lorettes*, envy the "ros-

series" of the *demi monde*, and live in a realm of *décolleté* silhouettes, *petits bleus*, cigarettes. Their "souls are cloths that one re-dyes with the color of his own."

The author knows so well all the haunts of this type of young woman. He can induct you into her alcoves, green rooms, trianons, temples of love. It is a vague and feverish realm whose confines are bathed by cytherean waves, and where there are "bals de rapins," "bals fin de siècle," and the dancing gaieties of the *peteneras*. It is a domain where the law of life is embraced in the question, What would people say? Its motto does not denote principles, duties, but pretences, conventionalities.

It is the world that Doucet garbs in graceful and piquant fancies. It is the world that M. Catulle Mendès versifies, and that the *Gil Blas* beguiles. It is the world that Massenet fondles with his langourous *cantilènes* and his titillating arabesques of music. It is the world that fringes on the *foyer de la danse* at the opera, where thick-lipped money changers leer polygamously from their monocled façades of insolence and irony.

M. Prévost has been correctly called an erratic Christian. He feels that he is in communication with spirits of the other and higher life. He is a spiritualist, a mystic, an idealist. Believing that the world is growing better, he prefers that it adhere to the good models and customs of the past rather than follow new patterns of manners and morals.

He is an immense believer in England. Its roast beef and rosebud type of virgin beauty are evidences to his mind that the Anglo-Saxon race will continue to thrive, and is destined to be present at the distant apotheosis of humanity.

At his Sunday forenoons in the Avenue Percier, one finds M. Prévost very friendly and cosmopolitan. He is a kind of enthusiastic young college man who is fond of discussing the literary and social questions of the day as if he and his guests were directly responsible for the progress of civilization.

Madame Bernhardt

Madame Bernhardt

In Paris, who has not remarked that hôtel with red window sashes in the Boulevard Péreire, and where a grotesquely-garbed negro bobs in and out? If we ring, the portal opens promptly. We enter — no one. We wander on, and up, four or five steps, and ring again. No response — no noise — not a sign of life. After a second sounding of the bell, perhaps a young Frenchman in bicycle costume will draw back the door, and invite us in.

If it is about one o'clock in the afternoon, we may just happen to behold Madame Bernhardt descending the stately, rectangular staircase from the lofty, light-diffused heights above. We watch her yellow sleeve langourously slipping along the balustrade, as its owner sighs and wilts and droops down the steps. She reaches the floor and, levelling her hand above her eyes as she tries to distinguish us against the sunny window behind us, she ripples forth in a key of lyric and pearl : "*Bonjour, monsieur* — I see nothing at all — nothing at all—— "

She approaches closely, recognizes us, and her murmuring lips change to an imploring key : "*Soyez gentil* — wait till I have breakfasted — I'm dying of hunger — *n'est-ce-pas ?* — I'm famished." And the blond, supplicating vision wafts through the door into her dining-hall.

We go into her *atelier*. It is her reception room. First, we enter a dark apartment hung with pictures. Then we descend three steps into her long, beautiful studio, which is bathed in a soft, aureate light. Here, at our leisure, we may explore and enjoy an æsthetic haunt of our hostess.

The walls have a faded tomato color. They are enriched by three conspicuous canvases by Clairin. The largest one is above the grate at the end of the room. It is her well-known portrait of the year 1876. In it, she is a frail, wispy *Parisienne* half-reclining on a divan. Clairin's second por-

trait here was painted in 1894, and represents her as some Théodora of a Benjamin
Constant — some Byzantine empress of
gold, tiger-skins and dagger-pointed fren-
zies.

Other pictures of her. A fine pastel.
And a little canvas — bearing the legend:
"To the Blond Dream — by Louis Bes-
nard" — shows the profile of her face turned
up and distinctly detaching from a scheme
of purple. Opposite, Spindler has painted
her in the style of Lefebvre's Laurreta — a
mystic outline of countenance ; a virginal
coil of hair falling between erect shoulders;
a myrtle branch in her hand; a background
of gilt.

Three or four busts in marble and bronze
repose on pedestals here and there. One
of the busts is signed — "Sarah Bernhardt,
Sculptor." This art collection is com-
pleted by a long, ivory-sculptured casket,
an inlaid chest, and several large reliquaries full of tiny Hindoo deities, gods of the
Pueblo Indians, minuscule Hottentots,
statuettes of Jeanne d' Arc, of Henry the
Fourth and of Napoleon, bronze turtles,

views of Niagara Falls and Australian cities. On a pile of these photographs, a pair of white gloves, hastily thrown off, lingers, waiting to be discovered by a maid or valet. There is a noticeable absence of books.

The two spacious windows are fantastically stained. Great tiger-skins and Spanish rugs stretch across the floor. The entry-way is flanked by two calla lilies, by two immense blue porcelain vases, and by two *jardinières* — one offering azaleas to the visitor and the other displaying big, fading, red roses.

A huge cage fits into, and forms a part of, the wall next the court. Through its glass side where bead-strung cords hang down like a curtain, we may watch a large monkey indulging in gymnastic exercises with the vertical bars of his prison. His neighbor is a green parrot. And above, a colony of brilliantly-hued birds flutter about and twitter. You hear an occasional cry of a wild animal, and there is suggested the odor of a menagerie and the savors of fresh, ferine flesh.

The perspective of the room is relieved by a palm tree. Behind it, just in front of and around the fireplace, is a more private retreat. Here a grand piano is half hidden away under the palm. White, soft rugs languish under our feet, and on one side a beautiful white silk couch with silken pillows tempts one to indolence. On the opposite side of the grate there is an enormous canopy bristling above with a display of mediæval weapons and heraldic emblems. An immense divan here disappears below a tumultuous array of cushions, satin pillows, eider-down bolsters. Underneath them a gigantic tiger skin steals away among the white rugs on the floor.

In this canopy the mistress of the house will recline presently when she comes in from breakfast, and converse, act, toss her arms and charm us beyond description in her rôle, not of Phèdre or Marguerite Gautier or Fedora, but of Sarah Bernhardt — the most consummate rôle of all. Interviewers say that no one in Paris, not even Sardou, can handle them as can Madame Bernhardt. She appears to make them

proudly feel that she is telling them everything. It is not until they prepare their
"copy" that they discover how she has
slipped around the interesting subjects and
piquant questions, and imparted nothing.

In her *atelier*, then, all is exotic. Hot
desert skies and burning yellow seas are
reflected here. She loves the beasts of
torrid forests, and the negro races. She
adores the barbaric — the pathognomic —
moods and forms of life and the violent
aspects of nature, rather than the placid
types of classic beauty and conventional
scenery.

Yet, with all her tempestuous career of
excitement and sensation, she does not wear
out or go to pieces like her romantic pre-
decessors — Madame Dorval and the rest.
It is because she is evaporative. Everything, with her, aërates into spumescence.
No dregs are left behind to do harm. She
cares precious little whether the Comic is
the expression of vice or whether the
Tragic is the expression of virtue. Tragedy
and drama are simply her pastime for earn-
ing money — *elle s'en amuse.*

In a word, she is romanesque, not romantic. And of course she has a secret horror of realism on the stage. She classifies and simplifies all that she touches. She has the art, too, of keeping young. She brings out dramas of the newest schools in Paris. She creates rôles of the youngest playwrights. She remains the courted idol of the Sorbonne students.

Yet, Madame Bernhardt is not like the poet Regnier of old, who is said to have written in his own epitaph: "I am astonished that Death should dare to think of me, since I have never thought of him." For, the cult of death is always a fad with her. She has had her monument built at Père Lachaise. Regularly every month she makes a pilgrimage to it in a rose-laden carriage, and with a wan and Undine coquettishness strews expensive flowers on the spot where she will pose and repose for the last time.

M. Mounet-Sully

M. Mounet-Sully

The saddest of all the sixty tragedians, serio-comiques, comedians, *ingénues* and *jeunes veuves* of the Théâtre Français. A fatalistic woe overcasts his face. He exists, acts, triumphs, yet lives not. Despair has settled in his eyes and left him only a fragment of vision. He plays the grief of Sophocles, Shakespeare, Racine, Hugo, but it is in reality his own grief, private, poignant, helpless.

Whence, the air of desolate pitiableness which always isolates him in any group of fellow-actors. He is a kind of haggard somnambulist whose intercourse with the world in general is unstrung in the key of elegy.

He is *chez lui* up five flights, almost in the roof, at No. 1 Rue Gay-Lussac, where the immense cheer of the sun and of the open sky whitens out a little of the darkness

within him. The apartment is railed in by
a cosy iron balcony which is decked, on
summer days, with a scarlet garland of
geraniums. The view is right out upon
and across the Luxembourg gardens, where
the Latin Quarter refreshes its gaiety on
warm afternoons and the music of a sentimental military band trails upward through
the harps of the trees.

In the salon of M. Mounet-Sully, bronze
Venuses writhe in their beauty underneath
the mute and stolid gaze of an Ethiopian
caryatid or slave. The walls are fatigued
with costly ornaments, portraits, gilded
crowns of homage.

By contrast, his dressing room at the
Comédie Française is an eccentric den.
Fancy a collection of swords, gauntlets,
green laurel wreaths with ribbons painted
"A Mounet-Sully," books, manuscripts and
what-not, all jumbled together in hopeless
disorder and with the dust of a decade upon
them! He will not allow the spot to be
touched. The various events and varying
epochs of his career, from year to year,
have thus left their mark of the moment

upon the place. The archivist of the theatre can read the *loge* like a histrionic sketch
or chapter.

However, this dust and disorder are
shaken up as often as M. Mounet-Sully
plays, for, he is addicted, on such occasions,
to habits of fury, vociferations of rage.
His *coiffeurs* are well aware that his finest
exhibitions of anger are produced, not on
the stage, but in private and for their personal benefit. It is merely a dispensing of
the bile accumulated in quarreling with the
characters who menacingly tread the pages
of his tragic authors.

These domestic scenes always end with
his hand held out frankly and amicably
and an "*Au revoir, mes amis,*" in token that
his white and splendid ire has disappeared
once more into that despondent darkness
out of which it sprang.

This is not saying that he is incapable
of amusing incidents. Perhaps you will
recall this one. Scene — a certain rehearsal
of " le Roi s'amuse." The music had been
written by Délibes, the composer of the
delicious ballet " Coppélia." M. Mounet-

Sully was filling the rôle of Francis I., and sang so wretchedly that Délibes cried out:

"It's impossible to go on with such a false voice."

"But, *Monsieur*," interrogated the tragedian, "how do you know that Francis I. did not sing with a false voice?"

M. Mounet-Sully made his début at the Théâtre Français in 1872. For a long time he was conspicuous because everybody found fault with him. He was too exaggerated and yet too correct; he was too artificial and yet too realistic; and so on. People smiled at the idea of his proposing to fondle live serpents while playing "Andromaque."

Latterly he has remained conspicuous in France because of no rival. The querulous public can keep on complaining that he rants and depends on mannerisms for his effects. They can keep on insisting that his physique is too fragile for the bowels of a profound distress, and that his voice is too frail to exhaust the lungs of a powerful rage. They can keep on grumbling because he does not tower down upon, and terrorize, the "first rows," and does not throw a pall of reprobation upon the conscience of the audience, and does not leave a deep, fatalistic echo resounding in the ear.

What of all that? Without him, France would have to-day no one to offer as a match for Irving, Salvini, Booth.

But if there is much to criticise in M. Mounet-Sully, there is as much and more to admire. We may note here two traits and explanations of his stage play and presence.

First, he is eminently æsthetic. The æstheticism of Racine finds in him the expression of its delicacy of mold, of its feminine charm, of its prevailing sense of the artistic. All this phase of French tragedy M. Mounet-Sully has been the first to accentuate and exalt as a reflection of the French cult of refinement and taste.

Then, as for the Greek play, he is an Athenian, not a Parisian. It is true that he was born in France of French parents, but he is a genuine Greek in spirit and attitude. He perks his head, strides

briskly, explodes quickly into wrath, like
Homer's irascible and boyish heroes who
wore their passions on the arm. His poses,
garbs, gestures are those of young Hellenic
gods — sculpturesque, graceful and superb
in a light and corky way. It is all exterior,
decorative. There are in him none of those
soulful depths, those vague profundities,
which characterize the north. And this is
as it should be.

M. Mounet-Sully is the last of the
ancient Greeks!

M. Coquelin Cadet

M. Coquelin Cadet

The funniest fellow in Paris! Who? Why, Cadet — M. Coquelin Cadet — younger brother of the great and world-known Coquelin! M. Coquelin Cadet is only heard of in France, but in Paris even the babies laugh when his name is mentioned. A farcical fellow — very — broadly farcical — almost fit for a clownship.

And what title and right, then, has he to be a *sociétaire* of the classic Théâtre Français? The best of titles and rights: by virtue of the Molière farce or "comedy-ballet" — than which no farce is more broad, more lively, more unbuttoned.

Imagine the decorous Comédie Française turned into a circus by the spectacle of M. Coquelin Cadet as Molière's famous simpleton Monsieur de Pourceaugnac, being chased through the whole theatre —parquet, dress circle, balcony — by a dozen

doctors armed with colossal syringes and
bent on performing that certain medical
operation so affected by physicians in Molière's day and so persistently ridiculed by
him! On these occasions M. Coquelin
comes up through the prompter's hole,
seizes a plank and whacks the head of the
first doctor whose bald and pursuing pate is
thrust up through the orifice — and this
disciple of Hippocrates is "laid out" on the
boards. Finally, M. Coquelin Pourceaugnac appears in a woman's garb among the
spectators in the second gallery, and is thus
able to bid a triumphant adieu to his perse-
cutors on the stage, and shake off the dust
of the *maudite ville* of Paris — *ce pays des
femmes et des lavements.*

M. Coquelin Cadet is not tall, but is well
built and inclined to stoutness. A prominent nose and mouth and very mobile features give a deobstruent character to this
physiognomy which the painter Friant has so
well portrayed — that broad exuberance of
visage with its message of prosperous irresponsibility and sedative hilarity. His
little forehead slopes almost straight back

from the eyes so that he can assume the look of a perfect idiot. Not quite perfect, though, for his two little brown eyes ever persist in snapping with intelligence and reacting against the natural idiocy of the rest of his face.

And just here it is worthy of remark that his gestures are never exaggerated. Quite the contrary. They surprise one by their extreme moderateness. His hands rarely fling out wide of the body. They rarely rise higher than his nose, in accordance with the classic Ciceronian tradition, and in accordance with the present fashions at the Conservatoire in its reaction against the ultra arm-flinging, hair-tossing modes prevalent in the days of Frédéric Lemaître and the romantic drama.

The *jeu* of M. Coquelin Cadet is, therefore, not only phlegmatic but severely correct. He will recite one of his monologues and scarcely move his hands from a pendant position. And yet one of the most popular diversions of Parisian society is the soliloquizing of this —

Souple et fringant valet applaudi d'un salon.

M. Coquelin Cadet is usually to be seen around the Théâtre Français. If you happen to be playing chess about dinner time right across the street in the Café de la Régence, the waiter is apt to ask you to be kind enough to pass to another table because M. Coquelin is coming to dine. And the next moment he slips in quietly, unobtrusively, with some fellow-actor, and hastily eats while busily conversing in a hushed manner.

For he is always in a hurry — always a little behind time. His *coiffeur* complains that he never has a proper chance to exhibit his art on M. Cadet. "*Mon Dieu* — I'm late — don't stop for extras; anything will do and anyhow," is his customary refrain. His dressing-room is, despite all his belated fussing and nervous haste, a well ordered, attractive nook — quite in contrast to the adjoining one of Mounet-Sully.

The special fad of M. Coquelin Cadet is pictures. "Yes, I have a passion for paintings — am a little like my brother for that," he will say to guests as he hurries through his elegant apartments in the Avenue du Bel

Respiro, and points out the canvases that are particularly precious to him. His two favorite living painters are, perhaps, Dagnan-Bouveret and Cazin — their *toiles* freely cover his walls.

Zorn and Roll, as well as Friant, have painted his portrait, and he has several amateur paintings by his intimate friend M. Waldeck-Rousseau, the eminent Parisian advocate. One notes in his drawing-room pictures by Sargent and Muenier, pastels by Madeleine Lemaire, and impressionistic paintings.

"Yes, I'm an impressionist, too — a little of everything — eclectic," M. Coquelin will remark in his hurried, noiseless voice as if he were out of breath from running. "And there's Sarah's bust of me — yes, in marble — well done, *n'est-ce-pas?* — *étonnante, cette femme — fait tout!* I came from Boulogne-sur-Mer, you know, that's why there are so many pictures here of Boulogne. *Tenez!* here's a photograph of myself — on a bicycle — yes, I'm a 'fool of a bicyclist' — only I limit myself to summer time. And here's another photograph — shows me when I am being shaved — funny idea is n't it? But I 'm done with all that programme now — I shave myself with that new American machine — it's superb.

"Look at that painting over there. Can you see it? Shows me as Isidore in 'le Testament de César Girodot,' my favorite rôle. Here's a picture of me in 'l'Ami Fritz' — the rôle that made me *sociétaire*. Yes, of course, I'm decorated — we all are in France. A young woman was saying to me the other day: 'A man without a decoration is like a woman without children.' Makes one laugh, does n't it?

"That big bust of myself on the mantel is Falguière's — and here 's a curious thing by Rodin — made out of some strange sort of wood. Gambetta in the corner — yes — I like that bust because it shows him as a man, not as a statesman. I knew him well — intimately. Here 's his photograph — can you see the inscription?— *A Coquelin printemps — Rire et bien dire?* O, I'm a republican — a moderate republican — not a crank about it, you know."

Tapestries, pottery, faïence, ceramics, sculptures, *tableaux* — all greet the visitor in the bachelor-home of our transient host. Above all, masks abound. One of the windows is painted with masks for its subject. On one pane is a picture of Coquelin Aîné with the words in French: "Prayer of Mascarille: I will rear my son in thy cult, O Molière." On the opposite pane is M. Cadet: "The Gospel according to Pirouette: Suffer little monologues to come unto me."

Thus M. Coquelin Cadet bustles about in an echoless way and chats among his household gods. These gods abundantly represent him as a *monologuiste* in salons, and in the clouds among the angels, and with the Gallic cock crowing out of the top of his head — Coq-Coquelin. And, everywhere — whether in flesh, oils, marble or bronze — he is always laughing and obeying the dictum of Rabelais: "To laugh is to be truly a man."

In this manner, this green, humble baker's son of Boulogne — smiling, open, generous to a fault — has made his way to

fame in the great world of Paris by displaying the *vis comica* with all the erudition of
exhaustless detail and with all the exactness of a variety true alike to tradition and
to real life — inimitable, indescribable.
Sully Prudhomme sings of him in a sonnet:

Quel bonheur! n'est-ce-pas? de réveiller encore,
En l'honneur des aïeux, dans le rire gaulois
La gaîté du bon sens qu'un beau verbe décore!

Such is the most famous monologist in
all Paris — such is the funniest man in all
France — this son of Villon and Rabelais,
of Molière and Boursault, of Beaumarchais
and Béranger!

Mademoiselle Reichenberg

Mademoiselle Reichenberg

Incomparably the greatest *ingénue* of our epoch! In 1868 she made her début at the Théâtre Français as the Agnès of Molière, and since that time — for thirty years — she has been conspicuously on the carpet in Paris.

The French, from Théophile Gautier down to the public of our day, have been completely captivated by her. She is the only actress in the Rue Richelieu who is always applauded when she enters the stage for the first time of an evening. The reason is that she is not only the *doyenne*, but is also the most popular actress there, to use the word popular in its most popular sense.

Mademoiselle Reichenberg has been, is, and ever will be nothing but a young girl — the ideal *ingénue* personified, incarnate. She has a girl's voice, a girl's laugh, a girl's gesture, a girl's disposition and ways. The

Parisians say that she is, on the stage, *la
perfection même*, for she is so natural in
her rôles that she seems to improvise them,
and then, too, she has in a supreme degree
what French actors call "style."

She delights the Parisians whether she
plays the traditional — classic — *ingénue*, or
impersonates the modern, half-freed French
miss who is capable of piquant enterprises
under the demi-frozen guise of icy timidity
and innocence.

I have seen Mademoiselle Reichenberg
in, I suppose, twenty-five rôles, and if I
had to choose among them, I should choose
her Agnès in "l' Ecole des femmes."
Here she represents tradition, nature, art,
in an irreproachable fashion. You may
scrutinize her in this part as severely as
you please with your lorgnette, and you
will find the rôle impeccable in its *ingénue*
timidity, fright, naïveté, correct spontane-
ity. Here, to paraphrase a familiar line —

Ses nonchalances sont les plus grands artifices.

As Marianne in "l 'Avare " and in " Tar-
tuffe," she has nothing to do. In general
her rôles are small, the *ingénue* being com-

paratively an effaced, inactive creature on parade without initiative or intrigue.

In modern comedy, her most popular rôle is that of the young wife in "le Monde où l'on s'ennuie." She has quite a chain of acting in "le Duc Job," for there she is a kind of free and enterprising American maid. Her delicious girlish witchery in "Faute de s'entendre" is the sole excuse for this one-act play. In this part she is, as it were, an *ingénue* in action — sportive, restless, full of pranks, crying, laughing.

Mademoiselle Reichenberg is — to vary the figure — the nightingale of the Comédie Française. First, because of her birdlikeness; second, because of her voice. She is a bird in flight — ever flitting, fleeing, skimming away. Always just disappearing or having just disappeared, she is never at home nor in her *loge*. Even at the rehearsals she rarely fails to be lamentably behind time and to cause her fellow-players to keep exclaiming for an hour or two, "Where *is* the little *doyenne? Mon Dieu*, how she makes us wait! — she is *never* on time!" At her young girls' class of recitation in the Faubourg St. Honoré, where she is supposed to give a lesson of recital each week during the season, she is usually conspicuous by her tardiness or absence. Only when she plays before the footlights is she sure to halt in a fixed spot at a fixed hour.

She pretends to live in a certain modest little villa in the Villa Saïd. A villa in a villa? The Villa Saïd is almost anything but a villa. It is a tiny by-way near where the Avenue du Bois de Boulogne enters the Bois. It is a short alley, and is lined with small, simple, one-story hôtels, all painted a lead color. At No. 21 is the minuscule hôtel of Mademoiselle Reichenberg.

It is the house of a little girl — a place where a lass might be playing at living. If you should ring at the entrance, perhaps a verdant English maid would appear on the scene, and say in response to your inquiry: *Madame est en ville avec son fille* (*sic*). The baby house is absolutely unpretending, with plain old tapestries on the small walls, and yellow silk hung over the microscopic doors. It is by no means rich in bric-à-brac or furnishings.

Her *loge*, by contrast, is a beautiful niche which has often been described, for, except that of Mademoiselle Ludwig, it is the only ravishing nook at the Français. It is composed of three bits of rooms hung in cherry plush. Its walls are covered with aquarelles and souvenirs of artists well known to the world.

One of the most interesting of these objects of art is an aquarelle, in the form of a fan, representing three mice trotting about on an ear of corn — an allusion to a comedy of M. Pailleron. The dedication on the fan is in the handwriting of Théodore de Banville:

> Reichenberg de tant d'or coiffée,
> Par son babil charme Paris.
> Car c'est une petite fée,
> Mignonne comme une souris.

Nov. 1889.

True to her flitting, bird-like nature, Mademoiselle Reichenberg has no fixed country haunt, and never leaves Paris unless she is to appear on the boards. If you chance to see her of a morning on the *plage* at some French sea town, you may know that she is to play at the municipal theatre that night. If she goes to Belgium or Holland or out into provincial France, her flight is only a professional one.

But she is not wholly invisible off the stage in Paris. Her admirers there catch a glimpse of her now and then at the Café de la Régence. This is the favorite café resort for the players at the Français because it is convenient to their theatre. Several of them usually drop in there for an *apéritif* about five o'clock. Joliet is sure to come in for a noisy game of chess, and Coquelin Cadet is apt to bustle in for dinner.

One day when playing chess there, I chanced to glance through the glass partition which separates the in-door section of the café from the outdoor part. To my surprise, I spied Mademoiselle Reichenberg's head, with its bird-winged hat, bobbing up and down and back and forth. She was charmingly engaged in a breezy conversation with a friend. She seemed a human nightingale in daytime.

Ever smiling, laughing, her face is never

in repose because it seems happily to reflect an innocent girl's conscience and a bird's playful irresponsibilities.

Being such a young ornithologic creature, Mademoiselle Reichenberg has difficulty in making anyone believe that she is serious whenever she wishes to be so.   A case in point was her attempt in 1893 to force the official withdrawal of M. Claretie, the amiable and excellent *administrateur* of the Théâtre Français.   She really meant to be very angry and formidable, and declared that either he must resign, or she would. But the Paris journalists gaily treated it as if it were a quarrel in a bird-cage, and described the *petite doyenne* as doubling up her pretty little fists and ruffling her dainty feathers as if she thought she was in a dreadfully pugnacious displeasure.   All Paris laughed, and, of course, she finally began laughing, and it ended generally in a sweet and blithesome twittering.

Her nightingale voice is an exquisite freak of nature.   Pages have been written about its pure, crystal notes, and its *ingénue* qualities.   It is the voice of some joyous and pearl-throated bird. To me, it suggests pearl rather than crystal. It is neither sensuous nor pathetic. The tones are so delicate and timid that one fears he is not going to hear the sentence finished; and yet they are so distinct, certain, precise, so clear and chaste, that you never miss an intonation — and this cannot be said of all the actresses at the Comédie-Française.

Her voice delights the hearer because he never knows what intonation or modulation is coming next. Take the word *Monsieur*, for instance. She pronounces it in a score of fascinating ways. Sometimes it is the piquantly balanced French monotone. Frequently it soars aloft, and descends in all the dainty chromatics of a complete vocal curve. And again, the last syllable often mounts in a delicious musical flight, and is suddenly lost in airy distances. The true charm of her voice is that she seems to have no control over it. Like a bird's song, it is instinct with separate life, and, always sure of itself, it disports with captivating faultlessness.

Mademoiselle Reichenberg is — to repeat

the phrase — the most famous and birdlike *ingénue* in Paris. She is the incarnation of all that is tiny, flitting, airy. She is delightfully at large and unconfined in the smallest of environments.

Yvette Guilbert

Yvette Guilbert

You know Yvette's history.   Here it is in a word.   She was a salesgirl a few years ago.   She was crazy to go on the stage. She had always heard of Sarah Bernhardt, and finally went one evening with her cousin (also a young woman) to see Sarah play at the Porte St. Martin.   They were so excited that they plumped into their seats without buying a programme.   Yvette was astonished at Sarah's poor acting.   Was it possible the grand Sarah could not do better than that?   Yvette began making comments of dissatisfaction and criticisms of disgust. At length her cousin procured a programme and exclaimed: "Why, it is n't Sarah at all — there's a substitute this evening!"

Yvette was grievously disappointed, for she had to count the *sous* in those days, and that night her money and trouble had gone for nothing.   She remained, however, and presently a gentleman next her, interested in her lively remarks about the acting, asked her if she was an actress, for he said her observations were sensible and apropos. "Why, no," she replied, "but I'm dying to be on the boards, and I don't know how to go about it." "You want to go on the boards — you are alone?" "O, *monsieur*, excuse me — I live with my family — a correct life — it's an honest ambition." He wrote on his card the name of an actor at the Gymnase, and advised Yvette to see him and get his opinion and advice. The card showed that its owner was a journalist connected with a prominent Paris paper. She never saw him again. She called on the actor, took lessons, tried the theatre at a salary of two hundred francs a month, and abandoned it for the café-concert.

That was in 1890. Now she is Yvette Guilbert. Now she is the Zola of the French concert hall!

She is a part of the great naturalistic school — a sister of Flaubert, of Maupassant, of the author of the Rougon-Macquart.

She is the first of the realistic song reci-
ters — first in point of time, and first in
that she has no second, third or fourth.

Fancy M. Zola a woman, his hair dyed a
fierce, ferruginous blond, his short-sleeved
arms rammed into long black gloves, and
his tuneless organ of speech intoning
rhymed epitomes of his novels — that's
Yvette! Still we ask, how does it happen
that a woman who is not pretty, who wears
a plain garb, who has no voice, who makes
no gestures with arms nor movements of
legs, and who simply stands on a little
stage for twenty minutes each evening
and recites four or five songs — how does it
happen that she earns 24,000 francs a month
even in Paris?

Eh bien! Yvette will explain it to you in
the following way, and if you do not understand French, she will explain it in English,
for she speaks English as glibly as a conversation book.

"In the first place, you see, I've got a
good head — I'm intelligent — that's the
basis of my success. I mean I'm not looking for a husband or a chance to flirt or

trying to go on the comedy stage. I know I'm not handsome, and I attend strictly to my business — to my art.

"Then I observe the world as it is, and I put what I see in my songs just as I see it. No café singer ever did that before my time. They were all singing 'My cousin embraced me,' and such pretty nonsense. They were not true to the great, broad life as the mass of people live it from day to day. 'Oh, but that's brutality — like the realists,' you say. Ah! pardon! no! — I save the brutality of it by my irony — it's bitter, severe, my irony, yet it gives a twang that makes one forget the dregs.

"Still, you must not only be intelligent to be a café singer — you must have *esprit* — that's what I've always had. When I was young, my comrades were always saying, 'That Yvette — it's amazing — what *esprit!*' There are plenty of café singers to-day who sing with intelligence, but they have no native wit. I am able to conceive the point and plot of my songs — it's I who find the idea — and sometimes I put them into verse myself, and I nearly always compose the music. Awful hard work all that — I have to think it and live it. Imagine the task of putting a whole drama or comedy into three stanzas, making every word count!

"And then, as I said, I have made café singing an art. With me it is not a sport, a pastime, a means to something else — I have developed it into a serious art with laws and rules. I say to myself, 'I am in it, and I stay there.' I've worked all features of it more than anyone. There's my diction. They talk about diction being a gift of nature. With me it was simply tenacious work. People have told me that no one, even at the Théâtre Français, has such a fine diction as I. And who, do you imagine, was the first one to say that? Max Nordau.

"You see, too, that there are all kinds of songs in my repertory — sad songs, dramatic songs, 'shocking' songs, chaste songs, songs of the people, of the boulevards, of the rich middle class. I can sing patriotic songs — anything. My dramatic songs — I can make an audience

weep with some of them. *Tenez!* one
song, I cried all the time I was learning it
— three months. My 'shocking' songs
— it's only the imbeciles who say that my
songs are 'shocking '— they do n't make a
distinction — they forget the innocent songs
that I sing for young girls."

And Mademoiselle Yvette's pretty choc-
olate eyes will glisten at you clearly and
steadily, and she will spring lightly and
nervously to and fro on her couch, as she
talks of these things in her loyal, earnest
way.

She dreaded her trip to America — she
would never, never have gone there if the
offer had not been so magnificent. She
was afraid of the Americans. She had
heard that they do not care for a woman on
the stage unless she has fabulous toilets
and a jeweler's-window display of precious stones. She had exclaimed to herself before going: "O, how they'll be
disappointed in me — they'll say 'she's
got no dresses — no diamonds — do n't
dance — she's not good-looking.' I'm

paid such a big sum for coming, they' ll
naturally expect me to be more than a
Liane de Pougy for beauty — that I 'll
surely do something undoable — turn myself
inside out probably. It 's horrible to think
how they 'll abuse me when they find I only
recite little realistic songs on the rigid lines
of my realistic art."

Indeed, one must not forget that Yvette's
plain gowns and simple, severe deportment
on the stage are required by her Zolaistic
repertory: that even her black gloves are
symbolic of the sinful, brutal, suffering,
earthly life of which she sings, and of which
Forain makes sketches.

It is to be noted that Yvette's audiences
in Paris are of the upper classes — the *beau
monde*. Last night, for instance, the Bar-
oness Rothschild, the Duchess of Ferrara
and such aristocrats were listening to her;
to-night the diplomatic corps will be present.
She twists a wry face at this, because there
is more money in popular audiences. The
masses swell the receipts. Of course a
person who, like Yvette, merely earns

24,000 francs a month, has a right to complain of such impecunious audiences as the Rothschilds and the Hirsches.

She has always had the press warm in her favor in Paris, for she has supplied a need created by the great naturalistic school. She belongs to her day and generation, and has sufficient brains and energy to march along her path with the leaders of this mighty literary movement. She was clever enough to base her art directly on life itself just at the time when the depravity and decadence of naturalism seemed to fill the very air with their manifestations.

To her, there is a profound philosophy underlying her whole list of songs. She cannot define or discuss this philosophy, for she never was a student at the Sorbonne; still she feels it, and means that her irony should be directed at the wicked and the fools.

There is one thing in which she differs from her naturalistic colleagues. She is not a pessimist. She believes that the world is growing better and that the future is full of hope. So she lives, not in a gloomy and misanthropic abode, but in a bright, airy, sun-lighted apartment, where countless mirrors and glass doors idealize the surroundings, and the furniture and furnishings are light and cheerful. She realizes that she has been treated well; she always lends a helping hand; she has not an enemy in Paris. If Thackeray were alive, he would perhaps epitomize it all by remarking that Yvette is a "brick."

Nevertheless, we must not forget that her repertory is not "for young girls." Some of her songs would, as the French say, "knock the legs out from under" even one of Zola's peasants. It is not Yvette's fault, in the last analysis. It is more the fault of the best classes of society who, despite their wealth, education, refinement and ideal opportunities, throng to hear her, and crave her feast of hard or vulgar realism.

M. Bouguereau

M. Bouguereau

In his Studio

A short, thick-set man of over seventy winters, with small gray eyes that twinkle fiercely when he is excited. His frowzy beard hedges in a kind face. His clothes are cheap, rough-textured, warm. He looks and acts like a farmer, not a painter of virgins. His rustic hands pasture nervously around the buttons and in the pockets of his coat. You would imagine that he had just brought a load of wood into town. At any rate you would suppose that were he indeed an artist, his subjects would be still life, substantial realities — meats, cheeses, cattle, hogs, sheep — not fragile, imponderable idealities, not dream-realms of candied sweetness and emasculated beauty.

He says little, guarding something of a good-natured, bucolic silence. After a while he clumsily lights a cigarette which

he happens to find in his clothing. It does
not occur to him to offer chairs to guests :
he keeps on his feet with every one else,
and ambles about in an awkward, unfamiliar
way, as if he hardly knew the geography
of his atelier. He does not articulate the
word *Oui:* he simply nods and gives grunts
of assent.

Nothing does he but paint from dawn
until eve, winter and summer. Painting is
his society, theatre, vacation. His canvases are his domestic pets. In becoming
a master — in preparing to create a whole
world of Bouguereau unreality — this gentle
woodman starved in Paris in the approved
art-student style. Often his food for twenty-
four hours cost him less than five *sous.*
Fortunately he was blessed with a rugged
bark constitution, and survived. Nowadays he shrugs his thrifty shoulders at the
memory of that emaciating epoch, for his
annual revenues are immense: his virgins
sell for any price he lays on their heads.
His house in the Rue Notre Dame des
Champs is commodious and commanding.

Well known is he in Paris for his kind-

ness and good-will. Many an artist owes
a "lift" to "old Bouguereau," as he is
familiarly called along the Boulevard Mont-
parnasse. He will go out of his way to
help strugglers. And yet so fierce are the
wars over new movements and art principles, that *les jeunes* affect to hate the
sight of the "old man" and to despise his
confectionery wares. It is astonishing
how much bile and causticity one of Bouguereau's pictures, with its chromo innocence and dainty-toned charm, will excite
in a young fellow of the "new school."

And when, in turn, you ask M. Bouguereau what he thinks of aëration in
painting, he will crudely take his cigarette
from his mouth, try to throw back his
shoulders, swell out his capacious thick-
waistedness, look you ominously in the eye,
and say with heavy sighs of suppressed
agitation: *Monsieur, tout ça — c'est la blague!*

If you were to step into the little glass-
covered side room where he works, you
would be apt to discover some very youthful, peach-cheeked model sitting in the
nymphic atmosphere of a hot stove. The

hardest task of his life is not to paint, but to find girls with pretty faces and heads — they are so rare. His faces must have instead of the dead, white, masculine color that M. Henner loves, a delicately suffused pink tint — that unsexed tint which M. Bouguereau has made his own.

M. Henner

M. Henner

A simple, fatherly old man, with a slouch cap, and a blouse as daubed with paint as a palette. His studio is in a great, gloomy apartment house, and overlooks the Place Pigalle. He enters and emerges from his mystic den like some solitary figure in a child's story of robbers. The *atelier* is bathed in a Rembrandt *chiaroscuro*. It is widened and heightened by dark, inchoate, dust-covered perspectives of forgotten picture frames, old reliquaries mounting loftily on each other, and similar disordered gods of a neglected household solitude.

On all sides of us here are red-haired, hair-restorative virgins iron-rusting in languor.

Now and then the lovable old master gets up, searches among his rubbish and obscurities for some ferociously graceful, iron-rusted maid. He puts her across a

217

chair in the dimly suffusing light, retreats behind her, meekly casts his eyes down at the floor, and says at intervals: "A pretty tone, is n't it?"—"Ah, a good color—very good!"—while our eyes caress the ferruginous *insouciance* of his wax models. He acts like an embarrassed boy showing his first attempt at drawing.

He talks of everything in the kindest way. "I like Italian girls best for models. They often have red hair, or can dye it red at any rate. I find them right here in the Place Pigalle. Monday mornings, about ten o'clock, all the models in this part of town collect in this square. They are ready to be hired for the week. It is difficult to find good complexions. I need solid tones —a clear, pale, even color—no freckled or cut-up tints—it must be *mat.*"

"It is not true that the nude has *never* been painted outdoors until to-day. Forty years ago I used to paint the nude in my little garden in Rome. I suppose people say that my pictures in which all the light is centered on a naked figure in a dark landscape, are not true to nature. But I have seen this effect in nature. Nature's light on the flesh under such conditions is more brilliant — splendid — than you would ever imagine. I once saw a woman bathing at twilight in Corot's pond at Ville d'Avray. Every ray of luminosity was concentrated on her. She filled the whole space. She literally gleamed forth in the vague evening scene.

"Leonardo has always been my greatest inspirer. Rembrandt is not a favorite of mine because he did not try for charm, as a rule. For me, the one thing in painting is charm. I put Proud'hon far above all the later painters [emphatic]. His portrait of Madame Jarre is the finest of all modern canvases in the Louvre. When I first came to Paris,— in 1848,—that painting struck me at once. It has been my ambition all my life to do work like that. Still, a painter must have personality, individuality. That is the trouble with the picture exhibitions: Everyone tries to paint too much like the others."

Puvis de Chavannes lives right across the hallway from Henner. These two mystic

idealists come from Eastern France — that
mystic side of Gaul which borders along
the misty heights of Switzerland and along
the obscure depths of German forests. It
is the Black Forest that is reflected in the
backgrounds of Henner. He knows and
loves it as if it were quite his native home.
Across its dark fringes and within its black
confines, he tortures in epic grace his red-
haired Fredegondes, Brunhildas and all his
other favorites of the fierce Gallic chieftains
and warriors of old.

M. Massenet

M. Massenet

The nights of "Le Cid" and of "Le Mage" were not of the ever-to-be-remembered variety. The music was thin, the epic dry, the *mise-en-scène* anæmic. One was reminded of much of Leconte de Lisle's epopee—of his favorite effete effects and desiccated grandeur. At the revival of "Le Cid" at the Grand Opéra on a cold January night a few years ago, Madame Caron sang in her arid style, and Mademoiselle Mauri danced. Yet the Jockey Club, between the acts, smoothed down its scissortails with unusually perfunctory solemnness in the over-heated marble couloirs and behind the swinging, silk-velvet doors. It was only a *succès d'estime*.

M. Massenet is, in the Paris of our day, the most popular living French composer. Its great world is not acquainted with M. Saint-Saëns, who is half the time far away from France, and all the time (according to report) something of an irritable bear; nor has it scarcely heard of M. Reyer. But M. Massenet! The word itself has a sensational sound and *bravura*. The public is familiar with this harmonist by sight. He is in touch with it. He is ambitiously accessible and pleasant to everyone, and knows how to win the Parisian ear. His name popularizes a programme.

When a band plays one of his selections in a Paris park, people nudge each other and remark: "It's Massenet now." If you happen to be under the cupola of the Institute at the annual exercises of award-giving by the Beaux-Arts in the presence of many of the famous artists and composers of France, you will perhaps notice that your neighbors passively designate all the musicians except M. Massenet, who, by contrast, always excites their buoyant curiosity — "There's Massenet — there on the rear seat — do n't you see him?"

What M. Thomé is at the little soirées of Madame de la Grange in the Rue Condorcet, and what Mademoiselle Chaminade is at the modest "musicales" of a certain class of Americans back of Parc Monceau, M. Massenet is in a far greater way in the music realm of All-Paris. He has endowed his country with "Manon"; he has written the finest French *airs-de-ballet* since Délibes; and he is a master of the *morceau-de-salon* type of music — a type which is, of course, distinctly French.

It is at Menestrals in the Rue Vivienne, the street where, according to Abbé Prévost, Manon and her lover stayed, that M. Massenet has his business office. Here he is besieged by veiled ladies on mysterious Euterpean missions; and by old and young men with new, marvelous methods of voice training, some of which claim the merit of making anyone sing beautifully at the age of eighty-five. And then there are those persistent creatures who are ever in pursuit of *billets de faveur — billets de la répétition générale.* O the perpetual requests for free entry! They are the bane of M. Massenet's life. I heard him exclaim one day that he had stopped composing for good, that he had definitely ceased all work, that he would never again be tortured by a rush for tickets for a general rehearsal. However, it appeared afterward that he was busily engaged in maturing, at that very time, two operas and, as usual, his varied balcony-garden blossoms.

Physically, M. Massenet has grown quite heavy. His hair is still dark and still brushed back, and his dark brown eyes are still effaced. He has a soft voice, a nervous confidential way, and feverish, caressing manners without grace or polish. He encourages and is enthusiastic for you. Full of optimistic indulgence, he expresses himself vaguely in interested attitudes and unnourished gestures.

M. Massenet does not pretend to voyage for the sake of inspiration. He had traveled in Spain, it is true, before composing "Le Cid," yet not for that purpose. It takes him a long time — often ten years — to season any beflowered and perfumed wealth that may have lawned his musical soul during a journey in a distant land. But some day the public is sure to be supplied with the baled souvenir of his tour — its math and aftermath bound into the form of an opera or a series of exotic *scènes pittoresques*.